A Time For Murder

The Victor Sexton Series, Book 2

Sammie Ward

Printed in the United States of America

First Printing, 2018

ISBN-13:978-0990450108

Dedication

To my family. I am forever grateful for the love, support, and being there when I needed you —Thanks a million!

Chapter One

Spencer Sterling watched as the helicopter land on the roof of WADC News building in Washington, D.C. His father, Montgomery Sterling stepped out and strolled briskly toward the mini cart waiting for him.

"I would like the private jet around seven-thirty," Montgomery said, making himself comfortable next to his son, Spencer.

"Where are you headed?" Spencer asked, driving the short distance toward the entrance.

"New York."

"Is there anything that I can help you with?" Spencer asked, getting out of the cart. He moved quickly to open the door to the building for his father.

"No. I have everything under control," Montgomery said, falling in step with Spencer. "Okay. Who is up first?"

"You have a meeting with Jimmy Farmer's attorney at two o'clock, and then Ginger Fox and her attorney. I just hope we can avoid any more lawsuits. It is proving to be a public relation nightmare."

"If we want to keep up with the competition, we have to hire more aggressive news anchors," Spencer said, pushing the up button on the elevator.

"You mean more people that will report what you want them to report," Spencer said.

"What is wrong with that?" Montgomery inquired. "Either they do it my way or hit the highway. It is just that simple."

"That was corny," Spencer said. "Dani wants to speak with you about Congressman Adam Barlow's interview."

"She's just as bad as her old man. It's because of him that I even keep her on. I have already made a decision about that story," Montgomery said, as the elevator pinged.

He stepped onto the main area of the sixth floor. "We are not running any stories on Congressman Barlow."

"Well just be considerate when you tell her," Spencer said. "Hey, Dani." He waved at a petite, caramel skinned, young woman anxiously waiting by her dressing room.

She was beautiful with a short, crop hairstyle. She appeared to be in her late twenties or early thirties.

"This is my station," Montgomery whispered. "I can speak how I damn well please. I am not changing my mind. I have invested too much in the Congressman to see it go to waste over a small scandal."

"Sexual assault is no small scandal," Spencer said through clenched teeth.

"Nothing has been proven. It's the woman's word against his."

"You know his history with women," Spencer said.

Montgomery stopped in his tracks. "Now look. If he votes the way I need him to, I don't give a damn."

"You mean you are blackmailing him," Spencer replied.

A slow smile crossed Montgomery's face.

"Good afternoon, Mr. Sterling," Dani McCall said, stopping in front of him. "Can I have a word with you, sir?"

"Hello, Dani," Montgomery returned her greeting with his own. "You look lovely today. Spencer was just telling me you were waiting to see me. Why don't you follow me into my office?"

"Great," Dani said, following them. She walked in the office to find Ginger Fox and a middle-aged, African-American man already inside. *Mr. Sterling fired her a week ago. Why is she here?* She thought.

Ginger stood.

"Ginger, how are you, dear? You are looking well." Montgomery leaned down and gave her a peck on the cheek.

"Monty," Ginger answered. "This is my attorney, Alston Albright."

"Mr. Albright," Montgomery said, extending a hand to him. "Do you mind if I have a word with your client?"

"That is up to her?" Mr. Albright answered.

They all watched as Montgomery guided Ginger to the other side of the room.

***

"What is this about?" Montgomery asked.

"I'm just looking out for myself," Ginger replied.

"Why not just come to me?" Montgomery asked. "Why drag a lawyer into this? Don't you trust me?"

"No. I don't trust you," Ginger answered.

"That cuts me deep." Montgomery propped a hip on the edge of the table. "If I remember correctly, it was you that deceived me."

"I cannot believe that you would sink so low as to blame me," Ginger said.

"Just wait," Montgomery sneered. "You have not seen low, my dear."

"I can't believe I had anything to do with you," Ginger said, walking out the room without a backward glance.

***

7

"You have to promise me that you are not going to make him upset," Spencer said as he and Dani stood near the door of the office away from Montgomery and Ginger. The lawyer stood near the window looking out at the street below.

"I'll try to be on my best behavior," Dani said with a smirk.

"I'm serious, Dani."

"So am I," Dani whispered. "This is huge. All the other networks are going to be covering it once it gets out. We should be the first to break it. My source has already confirmed it, and it is a reliable source. I'm just waiting for the green light from Mr. Sterling."

"Can't you just let this story go?" Spencer asked.

Dani focused her hazel eyes on him." You mean your father may not give me the go ahead?"

"That's a possibility," Spencer said.

"Why won't he give me the green light?" Dani asked.

"That is not important right now," Spencer said in a low tone. "I would not hold my breath if I were you."

"Of course not," Ginger said, strolling back to the other side of the room. "We all know that you have no power here at WADC. You are just an errand boy."

"Ginger," Dani spoke. "It's good to see you again. How have you been?"

Ginger meticulously threw her silk scarf around her neck. "You mean since I was fired?"

Dani lowered her eyes. "I'm sorry."

"You're a great journalist," Ginger said. "Just like your father. I looked up to him. He was my mentor. Do not let them push you around, because if you do, they will push you right out the door just like they did me."

"Get out, Ginger!" The voice boomed from the back of the office.

Without another word, Ginger flashed Montgomery a hard glance before waltzing out of the room.

"We will be in touch," Mr. Albright said, following his client out the door.

"As for you, young lady," Montgomery focused on Dani, "Spencer told me about you wanting to run with the Congressman Adam Barlow story. The answer is no." He strolled around the desk and plopped down in the oversized black chair.

"Why is it no?" Dani asked. "He raped a woman, and I think—"

Montgomery waved a hand in mid-air. "I do not pay you to think."

"Yes, you do," Dani interjected." You pay me to report stories that affect the people. This is a story that does just that. Congressman Barlow was voted into office to support the people, not assault them. On top of that, he is a married man with three children. The allegations speak to his moral character."

"How do you know that he assaulted her?" Montgomery asked. "Did his mistress tell you that?"

Dani blinked. She would never give up her sources. "His mistress? You seem to know a lot about the story." She placed her hands on the edge of the desk and leaned slightly forward. "What do you know about the Congressman?" She glanced up to Spencer who was slightly shaking his head.

A dark looked crossed Montgomery's face. "What are you insinuating?"

Dani stepped back. She realized that she may have crossed the line. The reporter instinct got the better of her. "I'm sorry, Mr. Sterling. I didn't mean to insinuate that you know about Congressman Barlow."

"You damn right, you are sorry," Montgomery said. "I just decided."

Dani arched her eye brow. "Just decided?"

"I am going to give your story to Marissa Prentiss," Montgomery said with satisfaction on his face.

Dani's mouth dropped. "Marissa? She is just an assistant."

"That's right," Montgomery said. "She is your assistant."

"She has never covered a big story," Dani argued. "This is way out of her league."

"Maybe it's time that she come up to the big league," Montgomery said.

"You can't do that."

"I just did."

Dani felt like he'd kicked her in the chest.

"This is my story. I did all the leg work and research on it."

Montgomery jumped to his feet." All the stories here at WADC are mine. You report them the way that I want you to, or you do not report them at all. The story is Marissa's. Just to show you that I mean business, I'm also suspending you for a week. No pay."

Dani could feel the heat pushing throughout her body. She worked her butt off on the story.

"I'm not going to let you get away with this," Dani exclaimed.

"It is done," Montgomery said. "If you keep running your mouth, Marissa will be replacing you permanently in the anchor chair. Now get out of my office!"

"You bastard!" Dani managed to get out before Spencer grabbed her by the arm and steered her toward the door.

"Give Marissa everything that you have on Congressman Barlow," Montgomery said after her.

"Dani, enough." Spencer pushed her out the door. "You are just making it worse."

Dani could feel the adrenaline pumping through her body. "I can kill him," she said out loud. She turned to see everyone staring at her.

Spencer let Dani's hand go. "You didn't mean that."

"The hell I didn't." Dani swirled around in her three-inch stilettos. "I have worked too hard and too long to get where I am. The ratings are up at this station because of me. Me! Dani McCall. I do not deserve to be treated like that, then to be replaced by my own assistant. How humiliating."

"You brought it upon yourself," Spencer said. "I told you not to bring up Congressman Barlow, but you wouldn't listen. The suspension is only for a week. You can go on that vacation that you always wanted to take."

Dani swirled around to Spencer. "You may be use to him treating you like dirt but I'm not going to take it."

Spencer stared at her. He looked as if he wanted to say something, then thought better of it. "I have a meeting to go to. Don't forget to give all your notes to Marissa."

Dani stomped to her workstation. Her instinct nose was twitching. "Montgomery knows something about this story. I can smell it," she said aloud. "He would not have reacted the way he did if he didn't."

Dani waved a hand in mid-air. Removing one pump and then the other, she rubbed her feet. She glanced over at the photo of her and her father, smiling cheek-to-cheek. Oliver McCall was the number one news anchor here at the station for many years before he died. He was the reason she decided to become a reporter.

"What did the old goat say?" editor Stacey Brown asked, walking up.

"He's giving my story to Marissa Prentiss," Dani said agitated.

Stacey's eyes stretched in disbelief. "You went in there hoping to get the green light on the Congressman Barlow story, and now your assistant is doing one of the biggest stories today? How did that happen?"

"That is what I'd like to know," Dani said. "I need coffee." She headed to the kitchenette.

Stacey followed. "Is Marissa ready to do a story this big?"

Dani picked up the coffee pot." Well, she is a great reporter. She has instinct. Passion." She shrugged.

"But?" Stacey urged.

"Like you said, she has never done a story this big," Dani said. "She lacks the fire and passion that is needed for this story. But she's pretty. I'm sure that Mr. Sterling will have a hand in what she tells the people, so I wouldn't worry about it."

Stacey frowned.

"I will fill you in later." Dani poured the hot, black liquid in the mug. "I blame myself for being over-zealous." She grabbed a Sweet and Low. She opened the packet, poured the content into the cup, and stirred it with a spoon. "There is more to this story. I'm going to prove it."

"How are you going to do that?" Stacey inquired. "It's no longer your story, remember?"

"I never give up on anything that I start." Dani took a sip. "You know that."

"There you are, Ms. McCall." Marissa's voice called from the doorway. She sashayed further into the kitchenette, her perfect pear-shaped bottom swaying side-to-side. Her low cut, blue, skin-tight dress and size C cup breasts was intimidating to most women. She was very intelligent. She graduated top of her class at Harvard. She was driven. Dani could not fault her for that. She wanted her job as lead anchor, and she may have just given her the opening that she needed. She could kick herself. But the battle was far from over.

"I just heard that I will be filling in for you for a week." Marissa was grinning from ear-to-ear." She ran a perfect manicured hand through her shoulder length black hair. Not a strand was out of place.

Dani was sure that if she looked up the word 'vain' in the dictionary, a picture of Marissa would stare back at her. "That is true. Congratulations. It is the break that you wanted."

"Thank you, Ms. McCall," Marissa answered in an excited tone.

"Don't thank me," Dani said. "I had nothing to do with it."

Marissa placed a hand to her chest. "I was sorry to hear about your suspension."

Dani let out a sigh. She knew the sentiment was fake as the look of concern on her face. "I bet you were."

"But don't worry," Marissa quickly added, "I will keep the anchor's chair warm while you are away. Give the people of D.C. something to really look forward too."

"Yeah, like what?" Dani threw back.

Marissa's face dropped. "Don't get mad at me for taking advantage of the situation."

"Look, Missy. You are only holding my seat until I return, so don't attempt to get comfortable," Dani threw at her. She looked her straight in the eyes. "You got that?"

***

Victor Sexton pointed the remote control toward the television in his office and clicked it off. He strolled over to the safe. First thing in the morning, he would take the club's deposit to the bank.

Since retiring from the Army a year ago, he was adjusting to the civilian life. Though he was co-owner of one of the most successful supper club in downtown Washington, D.C., he would be the first to admit it was not as challenging as his previous career—Commander of

13

Criminal Investigative Division. No job could replace solving crimes, chasing criminals, or being deployed on top secret missions at the drop of a hat, but he decided to settle down for his fiancée, Dominique Frazier. He promised her those days were behind him.

His military career had cost him one relationship; he was not going to allow it to cost him another. Dominique had resigned her position as an officer to be with him. He was not going to let her down.

Their lives were on track now, but things between them were not always so clear. The relationship suffered a major setback when, while investigating his last case, he exposed her uncle, Senator Harold Upton, his former commander, for having an affair with Lieutenant Tamara Hill, an army nurse, who was later found dead in the officer's quarters. The Senator's involvement in her murder and Dominique's best friend, Lieutenant Robbin Greene, were never proven but the allegation ruined his chances for re-election. He stepped down. He and his wife, Rosetta, moved to Florida.

Dominique chose to stay with Victor amid the scandal, choosing to accept his proposal of marriage. Victor could not help but remember how close they all were at one time. Harold and Rosetta were like his second family. He hated the way things ended between them. It hurt him to see Dominique so unhappy. She put on a brave face but deep down inside, he knew she was devastated.

The ringing of the telephone interrupted his thoughts. "Hello."

"Hi, baby." Dominique's soft voice came across the line. He could feel her smiling on the other end.

He could not help but return her smile. "How are you doing, sweetheart?"

"I'm fine. I'll be better once I see you," she crooned.

"Hold on a second." He pushed the video button on his phone. Victor's face split into a wider grin when her beautiful face came into view. His lower organ hardened, picking up on her meaning. "You see me now."

"Hello, handsome." Dominique waved.

He glanced at his Rolex. "How much later will you be?"

"Not long, I promise."

"Where are you?" Victor inquired.

"Out shopping."

"More shopping?" Victor mumbled.

Dominique chuckled.

"I will never understand how women can shop so much," Victor said.

The moment he said it, he wished he could take it back. He was about to get a how men did not understand spiel. He quickly changed the subject. "Hunnicutt is attending a funeral. He's out of town. I'm filling in for him at the bar." Victor simultaneously turned around in his chair at the sound of the knock on the door. "I'll be late tonight."

"How late?"

"An hour or two." His sister, Tonya, stuck her head in. He waved her inside. "I love you, too," he said into the phone before ending the call. He looked up to find Tonya sitting in the chair across from his desk beaming at him.

"What?" Victor shrugged.

"Nothing." Tonya crossed one long, brown leg over the other. "It's just good to see you happy, that's all."

"I'm glad you approve. When Dominique and I got back together, you weren't so thrilled about it."

Tonya lifted an eyebrow. "Well, I was wrong. Dominique is like the sister I never had."

Victor could not believe Tonya admitted to being wrong. An attorney, he knew how much she loved being right. He playfully put a hand to his ear. "Say that again. I didn't hear you."

"You're so childish," Tonya teased. She glanced at her well-manicured fingernails and giggled. "If it were me, you would have reacted the same way. You know you would have."

Victor looked affectionately at his sister, the youngest of the three Sexton's children. He loved her for being so protective of him. He and Dominique only knew each other several weeks before running into each other again in D.C. The circumstances surrounding their relationship was nothing close to a fairytale.

"You're right, I would have. "Victor stood. "What are you doing here anyway? I thought you would be out shopping with Dominique."

"I had to be in court this morning," Tonya said.

Victor walked around the desk. He propped a hip on the edge of it. "How did it go?"

"It went well," Tonya said. "We won."

"Good for you," Victor said. "Tax law is growing on you."

Tonya forced a smile. "I guess," she mumbled. She nervously adjusted the expensive, two-piece, five-hundred-dollar suit she was wearing.

Victor gave her a look. He knew Tonya had a tough time dealing with her new career. Before she married, she was a top defense attorney in Washington. She decided to give it up for her husband and two kids. He could tell that she wasn't happy. "What's wrong? You said you won the case."

"We did," Tonya said.

"Anything you want to talk about?"

Tonya lifted her chin up. "No."

"Are you sure?"

"I'm sure," she answered. "Have you heard anything from Dominique's aunt and uncle?" She changed the subject.

Victor took a deep sigh. "No. Nothing. It's been almost a year."

"I'm sure things will change."

"I doubt it." Victor didn't miss the sadness in Dominique's eyes every time she spoke of the people who raised her like she was their own daughter.

No matter how many times or ways he tried to put it out of his mind, he could not forget the day Senator Upton asked Dominique to leave his home after she made the decision to stay with Victor.

"They love Dominique. I'm sure they miss her," Tonya said.

"She chose me over them," Victor quipped. "Do I need to say more?"

"It's not your fault the Senator likes to fool around and knock people off. You were just doing your job."

"There's no proof the Senator killed anyone," Victor defended. "That was circumstantial."

"Only because Bradford isn't talking," Tonya replied. "A couple of years behind bars and I'm sure he will sing like a canary. They always do."

"That was one time I didn't like my job," Victor replied. "I wish things would have ended differently."

"I know you do."

"Look who's here," Gerald Sexton said, entering the office. He strolled over, kissing Tonya on the cheek. 'What's going on, sis? What brings you to the club?"

"Visiting my brothers." Tonya grinned at Victor.

"The brother that lost his mind," Gerald added. "Settling down with one woman."

Tonya waved a hand in mid-air "Whatever, Gerald. We know you are afraid of commitment."

Gerald ran his hand up and down his broad chest. "I can't give all this to one woman. I gots to spread it around."

Tonya and Victor burst out laughing.

"You are so vain," Tonya said.

"You mean delusional," Victor joked. "I said it before and I'll say it again, you haven't met the right woman. When you do, she's going to have your nose so wide open."

Tonya chimed in. "Nose wide open. Whipped. House trained. He will be a good little dog," she teased. "I can't wait."

Gerald rolled his eyes toward the ceiling. "I'm the one that loves them and leaves them. You better recognize."

"Like I said, delusional." Victor chuckled.

"Anyway." Gerald mischievously wrung his hands together. "Now about Miles' bachelor party. It's going to be off the hook. I know some of the honeys that are going to be the entertainment."

Tonya jumped to her feet. "Entertainment?" She gave Gerald an irritated look. "You mean strippers?" She crossed her arms across her chest. "If you are planning it, I can only imagine bucket-naked hoochies all over the place."

"What does bucket-naked mean?" Gerald looked amused. "Who says that? Besides, I don't know any hoochies."

"My husband will also be at that party. I'm warning you, Gerald, if I find out there are naked women there," she balled a fist at him, "I'm going to knock you senseless."

"What are you crying about?" Gerald replied. "The party doesn't even concern you."

"It concerns me," the woman's voice said from the doorway. Heads turned to find Dominique casually strolling into the room. She was loaded down with bags. "What is this about naked women?"

Victor walked over, taking the bags. He leaned down, pressing his lips to hers. He let out a throaty moan. "Done shopping?" He placed her bags on the desk.

Gerald frowned. "Oh, give us a break. Get a room."

"Stop hatin'," Tonya quipped.

Dominique peeped around Victor to Gerald. "What's this about naked women?" She walked over, poking him in the chest. "There better not be any at that bachelor party."

Gerald tried to look innocent. "I have no idea what you're talking about."

Dominique swirled around to Victor's lopsided grin. He raised his hands in a surrendering gesture. "Baby, I'm not in this. The only naked body I like seeing is yours."

"Uh, huh, sticking together like thieves," Dominique replied.

"I know nothing." Victor kissed Dominique on the forehead to reassure her.

When Dominique turned back to face Gerald, Victor gave a hand signal to be silent.

Tonya picked up on the conniving between her brothers. "Okay, Stephen is not going to that party."

"C'mon, let the man out of lock up for one night," Gerald said. "Won't there be naked men at the bachelorette party?"

"Wait a minute. Naked men?" Victor joined in on the amusement. He was not worried about Dominique. He knew their relationship was secure. He just wanted in on the fun.

"Jealous?" Dominique giggled.

"Of course." Victor chuckled.

"Good." Dominique moved over to Tonya, taking her by the elbow. "Let's go and find out more about those male strippers."

"You just remember who your man is," Victor spoke to their retreating figures.

"I'll see you at home later," Dominique threw over her right shoulder, closing the door behind them.

Victor turned to the bags on his desk. "She left me holding the bags. Great."

***

Priest strolled along the Ash Trail Pathway of the National Zoo in Washington, D.C. He stopped in front of the giant panda's cage of Tan Tan and Mei Xiang, one of the main attractions of the zoo. A group of elementary school kids were playing and running about. A teacher was recording the event. He was careful not to be seen in the footage.

Priest sat on the bench. "You're late," the voice said beside him.

"But I'm here now," Priest answered over his right shoulder to his contact, sitting on the opposite side of the bench, reading a newspaper.

"I never knew you were so spiritual. I assume Priest was just a name," the contact said. "That was your work in France, right?"

Priest reached in his shirt pocket and retrieved a pack of cigarettes. Removing one, he lit it and took a puff. "Is that why we're meeting at the damn zoo? To discuss my technique?"

"No." The contact snapped the paper close. "Is everything in place?"

"Of course," Priest replied. "You just make sure to transfer the rest of the money into the bank account once everything is done."

"Don't worry," the contact said. "I will keep my end of the bargain." The contact thought he had seen his share of hardened criminals, but none compared to Priest. He came highly recommended.

"You better," Priest said. "Or I will come looking for you." He got up and walked away as fast as he came.

Chapter Two

Several hours later, Dani found herself on a stool at Cadence Supper Club. She needed a stiff drink after the day that she experienced. The club was crowded as usual for Happy Hour. Admission was free for ladies if they arrived between 6:00 p.m. and 9:00 p.m. The women were out in full force, laughing, talking, drinking, and having a good time.

Dani looked around for her younger sister, Maya. She worked as a hostess. A junior at the University of Maryland, she was paying her way through college. She spotted her threading through the crowd, drink tray above her head, and heading in her direction. She was smiling and greeting the customers along the way.

"Hi, sis," Maya said. She sat the tray down, giving her a hug. "What are you doing here? Shouldn't you be on the air?" She glanced at her watch. "It's 6:30."

Dani swallowed the lump in her throat. "I'm not going on tonight."

"I can see that," Maya pointed out. "Why? What happened?"

"Nothing for you to be concerned about," Dani said in a tight voice.

"Was it old man Sterling again?" Maya asked.

"Like I said, don't worry about it," Dani said. "It will all be over soon."

"I don't know why you put up with him," Maya said. "He is nothing but a user. Someone needs to put him out of his misery."

Dani grabbed Maya's arm. "Don't ever let me here you talk like that again."

Maya pulled her arm away. "Look what he did to Dad. Here you are working for him."

"We don't know if he had anything to do with Dad's firing," Dani pointed out.

"You mean that you don't want to know," Maya said. "I remember things differently between him and Dad. He was accused of plagiarism, lost his career, and drank himself to death. Old man Sterling was right in the middle of it. But once again, he managed to come out squeaky clean and Dad is dead."

Dani closed her eyes a moment. "That's not why I'm here. I remember what happened to our father, just as much as you do."

"Working for the enemy," Maya said. "You don't act like it."

"This is all part of a bigger plan," Dani said.

Maya crossed her arms across her chest. "What plan?"

"I don't want to go into it right now," Dani answered.

"Hello, Dani," the woman's voice said, coming from behind her. She turned to see her sorority sister, Tonya Sims and Dominque Frazier beaming at her.

Dani's face spread into a wide grin. "Tonya." She threw her arms around her neck, giving her a tight hug. She repeated the same greeting with Dominique. "Hello, ladies. It's good to see you both. Dominique, you are looking well."

"So are you," Dominique said. "I enjoy watching you on television. I try never to miss a segment."

"Thank you for the support," Dani said.

Dominique plopped down in the seat next to Dani. "I cannot take another step in these heels."

"Shouldn't you be on the air?" Tonya asked.

"I'm on vacation this week," Dani lied. "Much needed time off." She glanced over at Maya.

Maya frowned.

"Of course," Tonya mumbled. "We all need to take a break and get away from it all. Are you going out of town?"

"No. Just staying in the area," Dani said. "Take care of some things around the house."

"It's so good to run into you," Tonya said. "I have not seen you in a while. How long has it been?"

"Much too long," Dani echoed. "Have you seen any of the other sorors?"

"I saw Crystal about a month ago," Tonya answered. "She's working at the UN in New York as a Translator. Tabitha is working overseas somewhere doing her UNICEF thing. You know she is big into that."

"I guess we are all doing what we dreamed about in college," Dani said. "Who ever thought the four horse women of Spelman, Alpha Kappa Alpha Sorority would achieve so much?"

"We did," Tonya answered flatly.

"You guys are sorority sisters?" Dominique asked.

"Yes, we are," Tonya said. "Spelman College. The class of—"

"Don't you dare," Dani exclaimed

Tonya's voice trailed off. "Anyway, sisters for life."

"I needed to hear that right now," Dani said.

"Why?" Tonya asked in a voice of concern. "Is something going on?"

"Yes, she—" Maya began.

Dani cut her sister off. "It's nothing I cannot handle." She flashed Maya a hard look.

A look of concern crossed Tonya's face. "Dani, are you sure? You know that you can talk to me about anything. We are sisters. We pledged to be there for each other."

"I know," Dani said. "Trust me. When and if I need you, I will let you know."

"Well, okay," Tonya said. "I better get going. I need to get home to the husband."

"How old are the kiddos now?" Dani asked.

"Noah is eight and Danielle is five."

Dani forced a smile. "You are so lucky."

"I think so," Tonya said.

Dani gave Tonya and Dominique one last hug. "See you later.

Dani waited until the coast was clear before scolding Maya. "Will you just keep your mouth shut? I told you that I have everything under control." She hiked her purse upon her shoulder and stormed out of Cadence.

***

Several hours later, Paula Sterling grabbed the glass of red wine, strolled across the master bedroom, and picked up the bottle. She made her way into the spacious bathroom. She turned off the lights and sat the wine glass on the edge of the tub. The candles placed around the bathroom set the ambiance she needed. Removing her light blue silk robe, she stepped down into the water. The warm feel of the bubbles stripped away the day's pent up frustration.

She closed her eyes to meditate a moment as she welcomed the silence of the house. She leaned forward when she thought she heard someone moving outside the bathroom. It could not be Montgomery; he was on his way to New York, and she wasn't expecting anyone.

"Hello?" Paula managed to get out. "Is anyone there?" Her response was met with silence. "Hello?" she repeated. A moment later, she let out a sigh of relief when Montgomery casually strolled into view.

"What a beautiful picture," he said.

Paula smiled. "Montgomery. I thought you were out of town. What happened?"

"The meeting was rescheduled," Montgomery said, removing his jacket. He sat on the edge of the tub. "Can I ask you a question?"

"Of course," Paula answered.

"Did you hear me a moment ago?"

"I heard something," Paula said.

"It could have been anyone." Montgomery poured more wine in her glass. "You didn't seem to be worried about who it was."

Paula chuckled. "I was not worried."

Montgomery began massaging Paula's neck. "Maybe you were expecting someone else."

Paula lazily turned her head to one side. "Are you jealous?"

Montgomery chuckled. "I might be."

"There is no need for you to be. I am as faithful to you as you are to me," Paula said.

"That's not saying very much," Montgomery said.

***

Priest drove the car to the address that was texted to him. He exited the vehicle and looked at the large, gated mansion. All he had to do was scale the fence.

With the quickness of a cat, under the cover of darkness, he made his way over the wall and across the spacious, well-kept grounds.

Priest planted himself outside a large glass window. All he needed to do was wait for his target to appear.

***

Montgomery chuckled in low tone.

"What's so funny?" Paula asked. "Let me in on it."

"I was thinking how easy it would be for me to snap your neck."

"Is that so?" Paula managed to reply with a nervous chuckle of her own. She turned to face Montgomery, still covered in bubbles. "Before you do, I have a much better idea." She lifted a long leg to his chest. "Why don't you join me?"

"I may just do that."

"You might just do what?" Paula asked. "I guarantee you will enjoy it better than snapping my neck."

Montgomery thought for a moment. "Hold that thought. I will be right back," he said and left the bathroom.

Paula leaned over the tub, picked up her robe, and removed the cell phone from the large pocket. She quickly dialed the familiar number. The answering service picked up on the third ring. "Can you please have Spencer to call his step mother? It's very important." She ended the call. "Damn it."

***

Montgomery made his way downstairs to the first floor. He removed the expensive tie from around his neck. It was a birthday present from Paula. He didn't want her or her stupid gift. The private investigator confirmed that she was seeing another man. He could not believe who it turned out to be. Once he dealt with Paula, he would take care of her lover as well.

He made his way over to the small mini bar next to the large glass window. The feel of the liquid against the back of his throat felt good. He loved the taste of good wine. He glanced around the room to see what looked like a man's jacket on the arm of the chair. As he stepped in front of the large pane window, the sniper struck him twice in the head. He slumped to the floor... Dead.

***

Tonya hurried into the D.C. Police Department. Since she had gone into tax law several years ago, she had not had a reason to step inside the police station. She was not prepared to get a phone call from Dani McCall saying that she had been taken in for questioning for the murder of Montgomery Sterling.

She was still reeling from the call when she stepped into a bustling room filled with police activities at eight in the morning. She bumped into Detective West.

"Look who's here. Don't tell me that you are looking for work?" Detective West said. "Isn't tax law filled with folks just evading the IRS?"

Tonya gave a false laugh. "Funny. I'm here for Dani McCall. She is a good friend of mine. What are you holding her on?"

"Let's just say that she is going to need a good defense attorney," Detective West said.

"Why?"

"Montgomery Sterling was shot to death at his home late last night."

"Montgomery Sterling?" Tonya asked. "The one that owns WADC? Her boss?"

"That's the one," Detective West said. "We questioned Ms. McCall and she cannot seem to remember where she was, and on top of that," he motioned for Tonya to step around the desk "the weapon that killed Sterling was found in her car. We're just waiting for ballistics report to confirm it. We seem to have her dead to right. No pun intended. We are charging her with first degree murder."

Tonya's heart dropped to her stomach. "As my brothers taught me, things are not always the way they seem. It doesn't mean that it's the way that it is. Can I see her?"

Detective West motioned to one of the female officers. "Escort her to see Ms. McCall."

Tonya made her way to the holding cell. She walked into the room to find Dani looking tired and ragged. She was the opposite image that people would usually see of her coming into their homes on the six o'clock news. Her hair was unkempt, face free of makeup, and there were bags under her eyes. She looked frightened. She gave a weak wave.

"Can you give us a moment?" Tonya said to the police woman standing behind Dani.

"I will be right outside the door if you need me," she said on the way out.

Tonya removed her windbreaker. She placed it on the back of the chair and took the seat across from Dani.

"Tonya, I didn't kill Mr. Sterling," Dani exclaimed.

"What happened?" Tonya asked. "The police are saying that you did."

"I don't care what they are saying."

"Well you should," Tonya said. "Can you tell me where you went last night after you left Cadence?"

Dani placed her head in her hands. "I went to another bar."

Tonya reached out and shook Dani. "Dani, this is serious. What bar?"

"Don't you think that I know that? I don't remember," Dani said. "D.C. is full of bars. All I know is that I woke up this morning to the police knocking on my door. They hauled me in. Then another one comes in and says that they found the gun in my car and that I killed Mr. Sterling."

"Was it your gun?" Tonya asked.

"I don't own a gun." Dani made a face. "I'm afraid of guns." She placed a hand to her head. "I have a headache. Can you get me out of here?"

"Detective West is a friend," Dani said. "I'll talk to him and see what I can do. Can you make bail?"

"Of course, I can."

Tonya reached across the table. She placed a comforting hand over Dani's. "Just hang in there. It's going to be alright."

***

Victor quietly slipped out of bed. He peeked over at Dominique still fast asleep and smiled. She looked so peaceful he didn't have the heart to wake her. The rumbling of his stomach reminded him that last night's activities never allowed them the opportunity to eat. He was famished. Naked, he made his way into the bathroom and took a quick shower. Ten minutes later, he returned to the bedroom. Dominique still had not stirred.

He moved to the edge of the bed and removed the black silk pajama bottom from the ottoman. He had let her sleep a few minutes more. He was not due at the club until noon. Dominique was working the second shift at the hospital.

He made his way down the hallway and into the kitchen. Being a bachelor for so long, he didn't own the latest up to date kitchen appliances as Dominique, but he did own a coffee pot. Reaching overhead in the cabinet, he removed a skillet and lit an eye on the stove. He began to prepare breakfast. To keep him company, he turned the television to the local news channel. He reached for the bread box when the anchorwoman said, "Returning to our top story. News anchor woman Dani McCall has been arrested and charged with first degree murder in the shooting death

of WADC owner, Montgomery Sterling. We will keep you posted as more information comes in."

"What? No way," Victor said aloud. He could not help but wonder if Tonya knew. The two were very close since college and were sorority sisters. He'd gotten to know Dani over the years. She may be a little high strung, but she was no killer.

30

Victor picked up his cell phone off the kitchen counter. He punched in Tonya's number. She answered on the second ring. "Where are you?"

"Where do you think?"

"So, she did phone you?"

"Of course," Tonya said. "She said she had no one else to call."

"How does it look?"

"Bad. Victor, it looks bad," Tonya said. "I'm going to try and arrange bail."

"That may be difficult on a murder charge," Victor said.

"Well, I heard Judge Charles Church is over the bail hearing. I helped his son out when he got into a little tax trouble, so I'm hoping that he will return the favor. I mean she is a pillar of the community. I don't think there is much chance of her being a flight risk."

"Good one, sis," Victor said. "Always thinking."

"Well, I learned from the best," Tonya said.

"Call me later," Victor said.

"I will keep you posted," Tonya said and disconnected the call.

Ten minutes later, the aroma of French toast, scrambled eggs, and bacon filled the kitchen. He filled a glass with orange juice. He took a rose from a bouquet off the dining room table and placed it in a vase on the breakfast tray, then headed to the bedroom. He sat the tray down and tried to nudge Dominique awake. "Hey, sleepy head. It's time to get up," Victor said.

Dominique raised the blue sheets over her head and flopped onto her side. "Leave me alone." She moaned. "I'm not ready to get up."

Come on, Nique." Victor nudged.

"Go away," she said and shooed him.

"Breakfast is getting cold," Victor said.

At the mention of food, Dominique flipped over onto her back. She sat up and scooted to the head of the bed. She leaned her head back against the headboard. Still half asleep, she ran a hand over her eyes.

Victor chuckled. He positioned the tray in front of her and lifted the lid. She loved his French toast. He always added the exact amount of cinnamon the way she liked it.

A moment later, he presented her with the single red rose. "For you," he said then crawled in bed next to her.

Dominique took a whiff of the rose's fragrance. "You are too good to me," She leaned over and kissed him on the cheek. "What would I do without you?"

"I hope you never have to find out."

"Keep giving me the royal treatment and you have nothing to worry about." Her stomach rumbled at the sight and smell of the food. She dug in. "Hmm. I love your French toast."

"Thank you. I knew you would be hungry." He winked. "Since we never got around to dinner."

Dominique smiled as she recalled how they spent the night, making slow, delicious love. "You are insatiable."

He kissed her on the tip of her nose. "I think I created a monster."

"Yes, you have," Dominique readily agreed. "What time are you headed to the club?"

Victor peeped at the clock radio. It was 10:30 a.m. "Around noon. We have a shipment of supplies coming in." He picked up the remote control and pointed it toward the television. Surfing through the channels, he found another station reporting the arrest of Dani McCall.

"Wow," Dominique said, chewing on a strip of bacon. "Dani McCall arrested for murder. When did this happen?"

"Sometime last night," Victor said. "She phoned Tonya to get her out of jail."

Dominique took a sip of orange juice. "I saw her last night."

"Oh. Really? When?"

"She came into Cadence for Happy Hour."

"How did she seem?" Victor asked.

"She seemed okay to me," Dominique said. "I really don't know her that well to offer much of an opinion. Won't she need a criminal lawyer? Tonya is a tax attorney."

"True. Tonya began her career as a criminal attorney," Victor said. "It was after she was married and the kids came long that she switched to tax law."

"I never knew that," Dominique. "The Sexton family gets more and more interesting the more I know about you guys."

"We are deep," Victor said. "I asked Tonya to stop by the club later to fill me in on everything."

"Are you going to help on Dani McCall's case?"

"I am only going to give Tonya advice," Victor said. "That is all."

Dominique flashed him a skeptical look before taking another bite of French toast. "Miss the action?"

Victor sighed. "Dominique, we have been through this before. The military and CID is behind me. This man is looking forward to settling down with you." He reached out, taking her last bite of bacon and popping it in his mouth. It vanished in seconds. Leaning down, he planted a quick kiss on her lips. "As far as action, you give me all I need." He jumped out of bed and continued, "I have to get ready for work."

As Dominique watched Victor get dressed, she could not help but think she didn't believe a word he just said.

She hopped out of bed and trailed him into the living room. He removed the truck keys off the key rack. "Have you given any more thought to opening your own agency?"

"Nope. We have talked about this."

"Victor listen to me," Dominique began.

Victor leaned his head to one side. "Nique."

Dominique stepped forward. She stood on her tiptoes and took his face in her small hands. "Listen to me, Victor Sexton. I know what you gave up for me. You gave up a career that you really loved."

Victor locked eyes with Dominique. This was one of the reasons he loved this woman so much. She was always thinking of others before herself.

"I was already leaving the military when we found each other again," he explained. "You know that."

Dominique moved her hands up and down his strong, powerful arms. "I also know General Goss has asked you several times to come back and work for CID but you declined because of me."

Victor tried to speak. Dominque waved him off again. "I appreciate it. I do." She wrapped her arms tightly around his waist. "But now it's time for you to get off the sideline and get back to doing what you love to do. I want you to be happy."

"What makes you think that I'm not happy?" Victor asked. "I have you. I have the club. That's all I need. Before you go any further, General Goss is no longer at the base. He's the head of some new top-secret government agency that he is trying to recruit me for. Are you sure you will be alright with that?"

Dominique leaned back. "Depends. What agency?

"I don't know. I didn't ask."

Dominique pretended to brush his broad right shoulder. "Liar. There's a vacant office next to the club that I think is perfect for your agency. If you don't want to work for the General, you should work for yourself."

Victor shook his head in disbelief. "I'm out of here."

"Think about it," Dominique called after him. "At least look at the office."

Chapter Three

The lyrics of The Temptations, "Treat Her Like A lady," pumping through the speakers, signified old school night. The huge crowd of patrons made it another successful night at Cadence. Victor did not mind filling in for Hunnicutt, the regular bartender who was still out of town for a funeral.

"Give me another one," the customer demanded, slamming the empty glass on the counter. "I just can't compete with her former lover. Some army ranger, special forces, macho type," the man said in a loud, slurred tone of voice.

Victor did not respond. There was a time to make a comment, and then there was a time to remain quiet. This was one of those times.

"Hell, I'm macho." The man hit himself in the chest. "I'm no punk. I've been to war twice." He weaved toward the young lady sitting on the stool next to him. "Hell, ain't I macho?"

The young lady, a regular customer, frowned and tried to move. The man reached out, blocking her escape.

Victor came to her rescue. "Hey, man. You can't harass the customers."

The woman quickly scurried off.

"I didn't mean the lady no harm." The man closed his eyes and placed his head between his hands. "I just wanted to talk. No one wants to listen to me. Not my wife, my doctors, no one."

"I'm listening to you," Victor said. "But why don't I put you in a cab and send you home?" he suggested.

The man slammed a fist on the bar. "No!" he answered in a loud, obnoxious voice. "I don't want to go home. I don't want to talk about her anymore. It doesn't do any good."

"Trying to drink yourself under the bar isn't the answer either," Victor said.

The man threw his head back, releasing a laugh so loud, he almost fell off the barstool. "Oops! You're wrong because right now, I don't feel anything."

"Thanks for telling me." Victor promptly removed the empty glass in front of him. "No more drinks for you." To Victor's surprise the man did not argue.

Awkwardly, the man managed to remove a pack of cigarettes from inside his jacket pocket. "Can I smoke?"

"No smoking in here," Victor answered nonchalantly as he wiped down the bar.

"No more drinking. No smoking," the man fussed. "You really know how to ruin a man's evening."

"Good." Victor came back with. "Go home. Work things out with your wife. Why don't you give me her number? I will call and have her to come pick you up. Or is there someone else I can get in contact with?"

The man waved him off. "No thanks."

Lyrics of "Who's That Lady?" by the Isley Brothers sent another rush of customers to the dance floor.

"There has to be someone I can call." Victor reached for the cell phone underneath the bar.

The man staggered to his feet and continued yelling. "Why do I have to repeat myself?" He turned and grabbed a young man by the collar.

"Hey, let go," the man squealed, struggling to get out of the vise grip he suddenly found himself in. "Take your hands off me." He punched the stranger in the face. The two men began going at it like gladiators.

Victor zoomed from around the bar and stepped between them. Three large bouncers arrived on the scene and slammed both men to the floor.

"Take him out of here," Victor instructed. "Come back when you sober up."

The man managed to break free from the Bouncers. He refocused on Victor. "Come on, don't be like that. I was just having a little fun." He raised his hands upward in a surrendering gesture.

"Well the fun is over," Victor replied. "If you keep it up, you will be banned from Cadence." He started back around the bar.

"Alright, I'm going," the man said, staggering out the entrance.

"Make sure he gets into a cab," Victor instructed one of the Bouncers.

***

"What is this about a fight at the bar?" Gerald asked, sauntering into the dark office. He turned on the lights and headed toward the desk.

Victor's long body was stretched out on the couch. His eyes were closed, and his legs crossed at the ankles. "It wasn't a fight. Just some drunk causing trouble. There is nothing to worry about. I took care of it."

Gerald propped his hip on the edge of the desk. "Not what I heard."

Victor's eyes remained shut. "Rumors."

"I'll take your word for it," Gerald replied. "What time are you heading home?"

"In a moment. I'm resting my eyes."

37

"Go on home, man," Gerald insisted. "Get out of here." He strolled around the desk and plopped down in the large, black chair. "Spend some time with Dominique."

Victor glanced at his Swiss watch. "It's only 9:30."

"You've been here long enough filling in for Hunnicutt. He'll be back tomorrow." Gerald opened the laptop. "I can take care of things here."

"What are you saying?" Victor sat up slowly. "You don't need me?"

"Not at the moment." Gerald's fingers typed through a series of screens. "At least for the rest of the evening. The night is winding down. I'm sure you can find better things to do."

Victor thought about the conversation with Dominique. He didn't want to admit it but opening his own investigation office piqued his interest. He enjoyed working in the club alongside his brother, but it didn't afford him the same level of satisfaction as solving cases. It was time to weigh his options. He would be his own boss, not having to answer to anyone and certainly not babysitting drunks.

He looked over at Gerald who was engrossed in his task. He was made for this type of work. He loved it. Dominique was right. People should do what makes them happy.

"Hey little brother. What do you think about me opening my own investigation office?" Victor found himself asking aloud.

Gerald's head popped up. He closed the laptop. "What? You mean like a Private Dick?"

"Something like that."

Gerald grinned like a Cheshire cat. "That would be cool. What brought this on?"

"Dominique." Victor walked over to the private refrigerator and took out a bottle of water. "She seems to think that I'm not happy running the club with you."

"Are you?"

Victor twisted off the top. He didn't answer right away. He didn't want to hurt his little brother's feelings.

"Your silence says it all."

"It's not that," Victor finally answered. "I'm used to—"

"Busting heads. Bullets flying everywhere. Dead bodies." Gerald finished for him. "I get it."

"It's who I am." Victor turned up the bottle. The liquid was gone in no time.

Gerald stood and walked over to Victor. "I know that."

"You don't look surprised."

"I'm not," Gerald said. He sat on the sofa. "I knew one day we would be having this conversation. But I admit the part about you opening your own agency is a surprise."

"I admit when Dominique first mentioned it, I thought she was out of her mind, but the more I think about it, it might not be a bad idea."

"I think it's a great idea. Especially since you don't like taking orders," Gerald added. "You should be your own boss. Telling others what to do is what you're good at."

"What are you saying?" Victor defended. "I know how to take orders."

Gerald chuckled. "You were a Commander in Special Ops. Commander of CID. You're used to barking out orders, not taking them."

"Whatever," Victor responded.

"So, you've given it some serious thought?" Gerald asked.

Victor sat next to Gerald. "Some."

"What's holding you back?" Gerald asked.

Victor ran a hand over his head. "Cases. A lot of private investigators I know are starving. I could end up looking for stray dogs and cats. I'm certainly not going to hide in the bushes taking photos of cheating spouses. That's not my style. On top of that, I almost lost Dominique once. If anything happens to her, I'd lose my mind."

Gerald placed a hand of comfort on his brother's shoulder. "I understand your reluctance. Dominique wants you to do what you are good at. We all do," he pointed out. "But that woman loves you. She knows the danger that comes along with it. She also knows you're not going to let anything happen to her."

"I hope you're right," Victor said.

"I don't think you have to worry about cases," Gerald continued. "Once word gets out, you'll be able to pick and choose your clients. Especially with a Social Media Expert like me on the job. You'll be turning away clients."

"You? What do you have to do with this?"

"I'm an expert at drumming up business," Gerald said. "How do you think we stay so busy?" he boasted. "I'm a genius at advertising. But that doesn't sound like you." He tilted his head to one side. "Is it me? Are you worried about the club?" He placed a hand on his chest. "If so, don't give it another thought. I can get Paul to help around here. You are part owner of Cadence, that will never change."

"How is Paul?" Victor asked. His cousin was medically discharged from the army after being wounded in Afghanistan. He was looking for a full-time job.

"He's completed his physical therapy," Gerald said. "He's about ninety-five percent back in shape. He's looking for a job." His voice trailed.

"If I open my agency, you will be able to put him on full time." Victor finished for him.

"Exactly. Or you can put him to work."

"That's a thought."

"Dad would be proud," Gerald continued. "He always said you were destined to help people in need. First, you did it by serving your country. Opening your office is another way to do it."

Victor bobbed his head.

"Have you thought about a location?"

"Dominique mentioned something about office space next door."

A slow grin crossed Gerald's face.

"What are you grinning about?"

"The top floor is completely empty," Gerald said. "Leave it to me. I'll make sure you get a good deal."

"How are you going to do that?" Victor asked. "Never mind. I don't want to know."

Gerald chuckled slightly. "Should I give the realtor a call?"

"Give her a call." Victor's cell phone rang. He glanced to see Tonya's number. "Yeah, sis." He listened a moment. "I'm on my way." He refocused on Gerald. "Let me know what you find out."

"Will do."

***

"We go before the judge tomorrow morning," Tonya explained to Dani. "If we are lucky, he will grant bail."

"If?" Dani said. "I thought it was a sure thing."

"Bail is never a sure thing," Victor said. "Remember, you are charged with murder."

"How many times do I have to say that I did not kill anyone?" Dani said. "They cannot prove that I killed anyone because I did not do it. So, get me out of here."

"What about the gun?" Victor asked. "Do you have any idea how it got in your car?"

"Look, I've already told Tonya that I don't remember how I even got home," Dani said. "I cannot even

41

remember what bar I went into after I left Cadence. It's all a blur."

"And you have no reason to want Montgomery Sterling dead?" Victor asked.

"No. This is obviously a frame up," Dani said. "A good one at that."

"Who would want to frame you?" Victor asked.

"I don't know," Dani said. "I mean, I report the news. I'm sure I have made enemies over the years. Besides, Mr. Sterling was not the most liked person. There are a lot of people who wanted him dead."

Victor sat across from Dani. "Like who?"

"Like Jimmy Farmer. Mr. Sterling fired him about a month ago. He filed a lawsuit and promised to get revenge. Oh, and Ginger Fox. He fired her last week. She showed up at the station with her attorney yesterday and they had words."

"I was wondering what happened to Ginger," Victor said. "I never missed her show. That doesn't mean she killed him."

"So, does it mean that I did?" Dani said. "Whose side are you on?"

"I'm always on the side of right," Victor answered.

"I'm looking from the side of the prosecution," Tonya added. "There is opportunity and a murder weapon. That is a smoking gun. No pun intended."

"But why would I kill him?" Dani asked. "I didn't have a motive."

"That we know of," Victor said.

"Then why are you wasting my time?" Dani asked. "If you think that I did it."

Victor didn't answer. He nodded for Tonya to step out into the hall. "I've seen people convicted on less."

"I don't think she did it," Tonya said.

"You're her friend," Victor said. "You have to think like that."

"You know her, too," Tonya argued.

"I haven't seen her in years," Victor said. "Besides on television. What are you going to do? You haven't practiced criminal law in years."

"I know. She reached out to me for help," Tonya said.

"Find her a good criminal lawyer," Victor said. "She's going to need it." He kissed her on the forehead and walked off.

"What did he say?" Dani asked when Tonya stepped back into the room.

"I'm going to be honest with you," Tonya said. "He said for you to hire a good criminal attorney."

Dani let out a loud sigh." I cannot afford a good one."

"What are you saying?" Tonya said. "I thought you said earlier that money was no object."

"I lied."

"You're a news anchor on a reputable station. I'm sure you can easily afford a good attorney."

"Trust me," Dani said. "The pay at WADC is not that great."

"Then why stay?"

"The opportunity," Dani said. "I'm one of the youngest news anchors in the country. My father started out there."

Tonya nodded. "I see."

Dani stood and glanced out at the morning sun. "I just bought a house. I'm paying half of Maya's tuition. It costs to go to the University of Maryland. Look, I just thought about it." She refocused on Tonya. "Why won't you represent me?"

Tonya chuckled. "Dani, I have not practiced criminal law in years."

"But you did practice it at one time," Dani said. "You were good at it."

"Yes. Years ago," Tonya argued. "I wouldn't feel comfortable taking on a case like yours. Dani, we are talking about murder."

Dani sat in the chair. She reached across the table and took Tonya's hand in hers. "You graduated at the top of your class at Harvard Law."

"I cannot believe that you are doing this to me."

"What am I doing?" Dani said. "I'm asking my sorority sister for help. I believe in you. I also remember that Victor was in the military and in charge of investigating crimes. Am I right? He's the one that you always bragged about, saying how good he was and how proud you are of him."

Tonya nodded.

"He can help."

"It's time to go back," the female jailer said.

"Talk to him, Tonya." Dani stood. "Between the two of you, I'm sure that you can prove that I did not kill Mr. Sterling."

***

Dominique walked in her bedroom humming. She quickly undressed and made her way to the shower.

Fifteen minutes later, dressed in a brown wrap-around sundress, she rumbled through the refrigerator to prepare something for dinner.

Dominique enjoyed cooking for Victor. She filled the counter with the ingredients for an intimate dinner of apple pork chops. A few minutes later, the kitchen was filled with the mouth-watering aroma.

She set the table for two, adding candles and a beautiful flower arrangement. Delighted, she stepped back and admired her handiwork. Now she only had to wait for her man to arrive.

As if reading her mind, she heard Victor's key turning in the lock. A second later, he appeared, looking as fine as he did when he left that morning.

Dominique met him with a genuine smile. "Hello, handsome." She bounced over, throwing her arms around his neck. She guided his head down toward hers. Standing on tiptoes, she pressed her lips to his.

He intensified the kiss. She heard Victor moan as he skillfully mated his tongue with hers, having her insides jingle with heated passion.

"Wow," he said in a soft breath. "With a greeting like that, perhaps I should go out and come in again."

"Wow yourself." Happiness filled her as she spoke. She absolutely loved this man, with every breath she took and every beat of her heart. He is her life. Her soft curves molded to the contour of his solid built frame. "I only want to show you how much I missed you and apologize for this morning. I didn't mean to pressure you."

Victor lifted her chin upward, locking eyes with his. "I should be the one to apologize. I'm sorry. I know you were only trying to help." He recaptured her lips once more.

Dominique wound her arms around his waist. "I love you, Victor Sexton."

"Back at you," Victor said. "And I have been thinking about what you said this morning."

Dominique's eyes lit up. She clasped her hands together like a child that had gotten her way. When she looked at him that way, Victor could not deny her anything. She knew how to wear him down.

"Really? You're making the right decision."

"I said I'd think about it. I brought up the idea to Gerald. He agrees with you, that I should be my own boss. He doesn't believe I play well with others."

"Your brother speaks the truth," Dominique replied.

"Anyway," Victor said playfully, "Gerald knows the realtor of the office building next to the club. He believes he can get her to give me a good price."

"That's great. See. It is your destiny," Dominique replied.

Victor laughed. "You believe that?"

"Of course." Dominique playfully slapped him on his firm rear.

Victor glanced around the room, taking in the romantic setting. He grinned a seductive smile, picking up on where the evening was heading. He really wanted to tell her to forget dinner and go straight for dessert, but it was her night, he would go along with whatever she planned. "What is all this?"

"I trust you brought your appetite." Dominique took his hand in hers, guiding him to the dining room table. "I prepared your favorite, apple pork chops."

"You cooked?" Victor asked.

Dominique hit him on the arm. "Funny. Just go and wash up."

Victor made his way into the bathroom. He turned on the water faucet, washed his hands, and dried them on the towel. "I went to see Dani McCall tonight," he said, walking back into the dining room.

"What are her chances?" Dominque asked.

"There is a lot of evidence against her," Victor answered. "I think Tonya is going to take the case."

"Is that a bad thing?" Dominique asked, pouring red wine in each glass.

"I told you she hasn't practiced criminal law in years."

"I think that it's admirable that Tonya wants to help out a friend like that," Dominique said. "It speaks to her character."

"Well, it may be admirable, but we are talking about murder," Victor said. "One mistake can land Dani McCall in prison for the rest of her life or worse."

"Not if you help her out."

Victor pulled out Dominique's chair, then strolled around the table. He eased his long body into the chair. "We're back to that again."

"We are," Dominique said. "Stop acting like you don't want to help."

Victor shook his head. "I haven't done investigative work in a while."

"Oh, come on. It's only been a year. It's like riding a bicycle," Dominique said. "I guarantee that it will come back to you. Think of it as a family business. You do the investigation work, Tonya will keep them out of jail. Sounds like a win, win combination to me."

Victor chuckled. "Me working with my baby sister. I don't know about that."

"Why not?" Dominique asked. "Tonya is a very responsible person. You said so yourself."

"She never listens to me," Victor replied.

"That runs in the family. But that's when you lay down the law," Dominique said. "Let her know who's boss."

"Oh yeah? Like that worked so well with you."

"When did it not work?"

"Baby. Really?" He reached across the table and placed his hands over hers. "Tonight, I don't want to think about anything except you and me." He winked. "The food is getting cold." He leaned back in the seat to prepare himself. Dominique lifted the cover off the platter of what was to be apple pork chops. It took all the will power within him to keep a straight face.

"It's awful," Dominique whined. She poked out her bottom lip. "It's terrible. I can't cook."

"No, honey. It's fine." He stuck a fork into the piece of burned meat. It was as hard as a rock. Dominique looked embarrassed.

"I really wanted the evening to be special."

Victor had to stifle a grin. He didn't care whether she could cook or not. "It's not that bad. It's Cajun style."

"Thank you for trying not to hurt my feeling," She stomped into the living room and plunked down on the couch. She grabbed the black throw pillow, planting it underneath her chin. "I can't even boil water."

"Hey now." Victor sat down next to her. He reached over, leaning her head on his shoulder. "Stop talking like that." His large hand began moving up and down her arm in a soothing way. "I don't care that you can't cook." Dominique looked up at him. "I'm not marrying you for your cooking skills. I will do the cooking. I don't mind."

"You can't cook all of the time. Especially, when you open your office."

Victor planted a kiss on her forehead. "Don't worry. We will work something out. I can even teach you."

Dominique dropped down into his firm chest. "Great. My boyfriend teaching me how to cook."

"I don't mind." Victor kissed the top of her head.

"What are we going to do about dinner?"

"We can go out," he suggested.

She shook her head. "I planned on staying in, just you and me."

Victor traced the outline of her long, thin neck with a finger. He followed with a kiss. "We can order something later."

***

The following morning, Victor was awakened by a flurry of kisses. "Wake up." Dominique stretched out on top of him. "You have a big day ahead of you."

Victor ran a hand across his eyes. "I do?"

"Gerald called. He says he has a surprise for you. He will meet you at the club. I have to get to the hospital." She got out of bed.

Victor tossed the blue sheets back and slid out of bed. He looked at the alarm clock. It was nine o'clock. "Why did you let me sleep so late? I missed my run."

"You had a long night."

"Whose fault is that?"

"Yours?" Dominique answered. "Have you thought of a name for your agency?"

"I haven't given it much thought."

"I got it," Dominique replied. "What about Victor Sexton P.I.?"

Victor frowned at the thought. He gave an I-don't-think-so look. "Sounds too much like Magnum P.I."

"Yeah, it does, doesn't it?" Dominique said. "I loved that show."

Victor didn't respond. He disappeared into the bathroom.

Dominique was hot on his trail. "What about VS Investigations?"

He reached over and turned on the water in the shower. "It has a ring to it."

"Yeah, it does, doesn't it?" Dominque said proud of herself.

"Unless you plan on joining me in the shower," Victor had a seductive glint in his eyes, "get out of here and let me wash up."

"Not this morning, lover."

Ten minutes later, Victor strolled into the kitchen. He was completely dressed in jeans, a blue sweatshirt, and Timberlands. He snapped the watch on his wrist. "I feel out of sync without my run," he announced to Dominique who was enjoying a bowl of cereal. "I'm out of here."

Chapter Four

Victor parked the truck in his reserved space, then exited the vehicle. He could not help but look over at the adjoining white two-story building. The property was built in the late 1950s. Numerous businesses have come and gone since his father opened Cadence over twenty years ago. He spotted the 'For Rent' sign in a window on the second floor.

The first level consisted of Stan's Barber Shop, Lucy's Cafe, Quick Check Cashing, and a Wash-N-Fold Laundry. The second level was vacant. It would be an excellent location for the agency.

A jingling sound caused Victor to look around. He spotted Gerald holding a set of keys in his hand. "Okay. It's a set of keys."

"Not just any keys," Gerald replied. "But the keys to your new office."

Victor's eyes stretched. "You got them?"

Gerald gave him a mischievous grin. "I told you that I would. How about we go take a tour?"

"This is your surprise?" Victor trailed Gerald into the building.

"Exactly. Unless you don't want to go."

"Lead the way."

They rode the elevator to the second floor.

The doors reopened. They walked down a short, well-lit hallway, and stopped in front of Suite 202. Gerald put the keys in his brother's hand. "You do the honor."

Victor slid the key in the lock, and it clicked. He placed a hand on the knob and took a deep breath. He was opening the door to a new life. It felt right.

He pushed the door open wider and walked in a spacious receptionist area. It was empty except for a circular Mahogany desk situated in the middle of the room. Positioned behind it stood a tall, matching bookcase.

Gerald tapped his fingers on the desk top. "You can definitely use this." He picked up a non-working phone. "This will be ringing off the hook in no time." He pointed toward the bookcase. "Nice. Looks like Mahogany."

Victor strolled in and out of other adjoining back offices. "No bathroom?"

"We passed it down the hall," Gerald answered. "Nothing a little renovation can't fix."

Victor walked into the large office on the right. "This is it. This is my office." He looked out the large pane window. The busy traffic and people bustling on the street below made it a perfect view. The Washington Monument stood in the distance. It reminded him of how much this country meant to him. He didn't have a problem putting his life on the line to protect it.

"Nice view," Gerald said, standing beside his brother. "Symbolic."

"Yes, it is," Victor agreed.

Gerald grinned. "This means you will take it, right?"

Victor nodded. "Most definitely."

Gerald slapped him on the back. "You made the right decision. Private Investigator Victor Sexton."

"That's VS Investigations," Victor corrected

"Uh. Excuse me," Gerald teased. "VSI. It has a cool ring to it.

Victor whipped out his cell phone. "Hey, I like that even better. VSI." Excited, he walked through the large four-room office space recording on his cell phone. He would send them to Dominique for her final approval. She would be ecstatic. "Dominique will be upset that she wasn't here."

"She'll get over it," Gerald said. "I'm sure she will have a hand in decorating."

"You know Dominique," Victor said.

"Hey, listen, everything is all set for Miles' bachelor party," Gerald explained as they headed back out of the door an hour later.

Victor gave his brother a skeptical look. "Gerald, if you have big booty exotic dancers at the party, it's going to be me and you," he said, stomping off toward the elevator.

"Wait a second, it's not like that." Gerald quickened his steps to catch up with him. "Trust me."

"Trust you?" Victor chuckled. "Yeah right," he said as the elevator door closed.

***

Victor and Gerald arrived in front of the building to find their brother-in-law, Stephen, waiting for them. He was leaning against Victor's truck with his arms folded across his chest.

"What is he in a huff about?" Gerald asked.

"I think I know," Victor said. Stephen hurried toward him.

"When my wife and I had a family, we agreed that she would no longer practice criminal law," Stephen said. "That she would practice tax law. She would not have to worry about defending scum bags. I would not have to worry about her."

Victor could tell that he was trying his best to remain calm.

"Then she comes home last night and tells me that she is going to represent Dani McCall. What is that all about? Did you talk her into it?" he asked, looking directly at Victor.

"What makes you think that I talked her into it?" Victor said. "I told Tonya that I thought that she should give Dani McCall's case to another lawyer."

"Wait a minute," Gerald said. "Tonya is taking the Dani McCall case? When did this happen? And why no one told me?"

"Yesterday," Victor answered. He refocused back on Stephen. "Tonya is taking the case?"

"She didn't listen to you," Stephen said. "She already left this morning for the bail hearing."

"I need to get down to the court house." Victor rushed toward the truck.

"What?" Stephen said. "You are in on this, too?"

Victor stopped in mid-stride. "Look, Stephen, if Tonya insists on doing this, wouldn't you like me to have her back? You know Dani and Tonya are sorority sisters, right? I have a feeling she's not going to listen to either one of us on this one."

Stephen dipped his head a moment.

"Besides, Victor is getting ready to open his own private investigation agency," Gerald threw in. "We both know that he is more than capable to look after Tonya. There is no need to worry. Brother-in-law, you are into renovation, right?" he asked, changing the subject.

"You know I am," Stephen said.

"Good. Come and see the future home of VSI. We will need your expertise on some things." Victor heard Gerald say as they walked away. Victor hopped in the truck and pulled out of the parking lot.

***

"The bail hearing went well," Tonya said, strolling to a barstool several hours later. She removed her pumps and placed her Michael Kors large bag on the counter. "The judge set it at three hundred and fifty thousand dollars."

Victor zoomed behind the counter. "Does Ms. McCall have that kind of money?"

"She put up her house for collateral," Tonya said, rubbing her feet.

"I know I keep asking you this, but are you sure you want to take on this case?" Victor grabbed a hand full of peanuts and popped them in his mouth. "You are personally involved and that is never a good thing."

"That's why I need you," Tonya said. "Look, I was thinking that maybe we should work together on this one. I need a second set of eyes. The prosecuting attorney is Stephanie Bigelow."

"Is she good?" Victor asked.

"Is she good?" Tonya repeated. "They don't call her a barracuda for nothing. She's one of the best. I have to be on my game."

"You want to hire me?"

Tonya frowned. "Hire you? You're my brother. You should be willing to do it for free."

"I'm a brother that just opened an investigations agency," Victor explained. "If I decide to take the McCall case, it will be the first for the agency."

Tonya leaned back. "A private investigation agency?"

"Yep."

"Do you have a license to run an agency?"

"That is just a formality."

Tonya chuckled. "What is the name of this agency? What is the fee?" She waved a hand in mid-air. "Where is it?"

"The name of the agency is VSI," Victor said. "Which stands for Victor Sexton Investigations. I haven't decided on the fee yet, but I will get back to you on that." He had to admit that the sound of his own investigation service sounds good rolling off his tongue. "I'm taking an office on the second floor of the building next door. Suite 202."

"Hmm," Tonya said. "Sounds good. You're more than qualified. I like the location."

Gerald appeared from the back. "I even took him over for a quick tour. Your husband also looked around. I even got him to help with some of the renovations."

"Stephen?" Tonya asked in surprise.

"Yes, Stephen," Gerald imitated.

"What does Dominique think about all of this?" Tonya inquired.

"It was Dominique that suggested it, "Victor said, placing a bottle of beer in front of her. "Am I hired?"

"Of, course you are," Tonya said. "Was there ever any doubt? Is there a contract?" she teased.

"Give me a break," Victor said. "You are my first client." He extended a hand to his sister. "For now, let's shake on it."

"All right," Tonya said, accepting her brother's handshake. "Where do we start?"

"We start?" Victor repeated.

"Yes," Tonya said. "I'm working with you."

The brothers chuckled.

She gave then a side-eye. "What's so funny?"

"One. You don't know the first thing about investigative work," Victor said. "That's why you just hired me. I do the investigating. You do the defending."

"Two. You might break a nail or something," Gerald added. "Let him do the leg work."

"I know a lot about interviewing people." She defended herself as she stared at Victor.

"So, do I," Victor countered.

"Anyway, I want to interview Mrs. Sterling," she said.

"I don't think so," Victor said. "I will investigate Mrs. Sterling."

"I don't appreciate you two knuckleheads disrespecting me like this," Tonya said with attitude. "I'm Dani's attorney.

I'm trying to get her off on a murder charge. I want to talk to Mrs. Sterling and see what she knows. I've heard all sorts of rumors about their marriage. Speaking with the wife may give me a chance to know if those rumors are true or not."

"What kind of rumors?" Victor asked.

Tonya pointed at Victor. "You don't know anything, do you? For someone that owns the hottest club in the district, you are in the dark about what is going on in this city."

"Part owner," Gerald corrected.

Victor sighed. "Whatever. Just tell me the rumor."

"Well, she's a lot younger than Mr. Sterling, and she had to sign a prenuptial agreement."

"Lots of couples these days sign a prenup," Victor said. "It doesn't mean anything." He thought a moment. "I would be curious to know the conditions surrounding it."

"I heard that she gets a million dollar for every year that she is married to him," Gerald said. "He can divorce her, but if she divorces him then she gets nothing."

Tonya and Victor gave Gerald a look.

"What? I know what is going on in this town," Gerald said. "It's my business to know."

Victor rubbed a hand underneath his chin. "Interesting."

"I hope the rumors about the open marriage is true," Gerald continued. "Mrs. Sterling is fine. Can I go with you when you interview her?"

"No!" Tonya and Victor answered in unison.

"Gerald, can you do me a favor?" Tonya asked.

"What's that?"

"Can you pick up Dani McCall from the police station and bring her back here?" Tonya asked. "I need to set some ground rules for her to follow while she is out on bail, so make sure that she stays here until we get back." She stepped down in one pump than the other and adjusted her two-piece, tan skirt suit.

"I see," Gerald complained. "I can't go see the lovely Mrs. Sterling, but I'm a taxi service and babysitter for the suspect. Great."

"Thank you, Gerald," Tonya teased. "Come on, Victor. Let's go."

"You drive." Victor went to the passenger door of the blue Mercedes. "I'll need all the notes that you have on this case."

Tonya reached inside the bag and slid a brown folder across the top of the car. "Knock yourself out. A copy of the police report and photos of the crime scene is also in there." She unarmed the vehicle, opened the door, and pushed the ignition button.

Victor grabbed the folder. He slid his long frame in the passenger seat with ease.

Tonya skillfully maneuvered the vehicle out into the flow of traffic. "Thanks again for helping me with this case."

"You knew that I would." Victor began reading the reports. "What about the time of death?"

"I didn't know for sure." Tonya stopped at the light at the end of the street. "But I was hoping you would. I'm glad that Dominique pushed you to open your own agency. I finally get a chance to work with my big brother." She smiled over at Victor. "This is a dream come true for me. The medical examiner puts the time of death between nine and eleven p.m. last night."

"As long as you follow the rules and do what I say," Victor said. "We will get along just fine."

"Of course." Tonya made a right turn.

"You might want to have a word with Stephen," Victor said. "Calm him down."

"Why?" Tonya asked. "Did he say something to you?"

"When he spoke with me and Gerald this morning, he was a little upset about you taking this case," Victor said. "That's how I found out about the bail hearing this morning."

Tonya kept her eyes on the road. She didn't respond.

Victor looked up. "Is everything alright?"

"It will be," Tonya said. "We had a discussion this morning."

"A discussion?"

"A heated discussion," Tonya admitted.

"Tonya, if this is going to cause problems in your marriage…" Victor began.

"I am not going to turn my back on a friend." Tonya glanced over at Victor. "Don't worry about it."

"What do you mean, don't worry about it?" Victor asked. "I know something about what you are going through."

"And you and Dominique got through it."

"And we are still going through it," Victor argued.

"I know you mean well but I cannot talk about this now," Tonya said. "Can we just concentrate on the case?"

"If you say so," Victor said. "Where are we headed?" He glanced out the window.

"Chevy Chase."

"We should have made a left back at the light and got on the interstate," Victor said. "It's faster."

"No. Taking this street all the way out is faster," Tonya argued.

"Left."

"Right," Tonya threw back. "I know where I am going."

"Didn't you just agree that you were going to do everything I say?" Victor asked, when Tonya overtook a vehicle.

"Did I?" Tonya asked, stepping down on the gas. "I don't remember that."

***

"We finally made it," Tonya said, an hour later.

"If we would have taken that left and got on the interstate, we would have gotten here sooner."

"You're still talking about that?"

"Yes, I am."

Tonya pulled the car up to a gated mansion. "It must be nice to live the good life. Look at that house."

"To live the good life is not all that it's cracked up to be."

"Who do you think framed Dani? The suspect list consists of about one hundred people." Tonya pushed the intercom system.

"Yes," the deep, male voice answered.

"Attorney Tonya Sims and associate to see Mrs. Sterling."

A moment later the gate slowly began to open. Tonya drove the long winding road toward the house. "Where do we start?"

"After Mrs. Sterling, we will want to talk with Jimmy Farmer and Ginger Fox," Victor said. "According to Dani, both have motives to kill old man Sterling."

Tonya parked behind several other vehicles and exited the car.

"I thought the police secured the murder scene," Victor said, looking out the windshield. "No one is supposed to be here."

"I guess they didn't get the memo," Tonya said.

Victor fell in step with Tonya. "Let's go tell them."

"The plan hasn't changed," Tonya said. "I will speak with Mrs. Sterling. You look around outside."

"Fine," Victor said. "We'll meet up later."

***

Tonya walked up to the large, round-set double doors. She grabbed the corpulent, gold lion handle and knocked. A few minutes later, a thin, middle aged, white haired man appeared and escorted her inside the foyer. "Are you attorney Sims?"

"Yes, I am."

"Come this way, please. Mrs. Sterling is waiting for you."

Tonya followed the man down a short hallway. He led her to a room on the right. She expected to see a woman grieving. Instead she found her surrounded by what looks like employees and she was barking out orders.

"I want those numbers by the end of the day," Mrs. Sterling said to one woman.

"Yes, ma'am," the woman said in a timid voice.

"This is a murder scene," Tonya said, strolling further in the room. "No one is supposed to be here."

"Who are you?" Mrs. Sterling asked.

"My name is Tonya Sims. I'm the Attorney for Dani McCall." Tonya could hear the whispers around the room.

"Why don't you guys step out a moment?" Mrs. Sterling instructed.

"I will repeat myself," Tonya said. "This is a crime scene, which means the mansion is closed until further notice. Leave or I'll place a call to Detective West."

The group of workers got up and left the room quietly.

Tonya refocused on Mrs. Sterling. "Mrs. Sterling, Except for wearing that black dress, you do not appear to be grieving at all."

"It wasn't their fault. I asked them to come out. Would you like some coffee?" Mrs. Sterling asked.

"No, thank you," Tonya said. She didn't know what to expect from the widow of Montgomery Sterling. He was

62-years-old. She was his third wife. She looks to be in her mid-thirties. Besides from money, she didn't see what they could have in common.

"If I were to tell you that our marriage was based on true love, you would know that I was lying," she said, pouring hot liquid in a cup. "But we were good friends."

"I see," Tonya said.

"I'm trying to be honest," Mrs. Sterling said.

"That is refreshing," Tonya said. "I appreciate it, even if I do not believe it to be true."

"I have no reason to lie."

"I cannot take your word for it."

"Does this mean that I am a suspect in my husband's murder?" Mrs. Sterling said. "I have always wanted to be considered a suspect in a murder case."

"I'll keep that in mind," Tonya said. "Before you married your late husband, there was rumors about a prenuptial agreement."

"I'm sure that you will find out they were not rumors," Mrs. Sterling said. "The agreement says that I get a million dollar a year for every year that we are married. If my husband divorces me, I get nothing. Talk about being on a leash."

"What about the mistress?"

Mrs. Sterling chuckled. "What about her? There was always a new fling. We had that kind of marriage, but that was also common knowledge."

"I heard he was serious about the latest mistress."

"He always strayed," Mrs. Sterling said. "But he always came back home, like the good little dog that he was. Now if there is nothing else, we are done."

"That's all for now," Tonya said. "I'm sure that we'll speak again. I can see myself out."

A few minutes later, Tonya found Victor on the right side of the house. Yellow police tape marked off the area where the murder took place. He was using his cell phone to take additional photos of the crime scene where Montgomery Sterling was shot.

"Sis, can you go over to where the killer stood?" Victor barked over his right shoulder.

"How did you know it was me?" Tonya asked, walking over to a spot just beyond the wall.

"The sounds of your shoes," Victor said. "Now this is the window the police marked as the spot where Sterling was standing when he was shot. How far apart are we?"

"About twenty yards."

"Okay, you can come over now." Victor began slowly walking up and down. "Now according to the police report, he had just poured himself a drink. He was moving around."

"Like you are doing?" Tonya asked.

"Two precise shots in the head by the killer brought him down from twenty-yards away. It was done through curtains. Amazing," Victor said.

"What are you saying? The killer was a hired gun?" Tonya asked.

"It appears to be expertly planned and executed," Victor said. "That can only be done by a professional."

Tonya sighed. "Which means that any of the suspects could have hired the killer."

"Correct," Victor said. "Even if they had an alibi at the time of the murder, they could also be guilty."

"That includes Dani," Tonya said.

"I'm afraid so," Victor answered. "Come on, let's head back. I need to stop by and see Detective West. Get an accurate time from the coroner."

"What for?"

"I want to take a look at the body," Victor said. "What did you find out from Mrs. Sterling?"

"That she is not grieving," Tonya said.

"Oh?" Victor looked confused. "What do you mean?"

"She was carrying on with business as usual," Tonya said. "She said that if she was to grieve that it would be a lie."

"At least she's honest," Victor said.

"And she's at the top of our suspect list," Tonya replied.

"Without a doubt," Victor agreed. "The spouse is always looked at first."

Chapter Five

Tonya dropped Victor off in front of Cadence. He hopped in his truck and headed to the Police Department. Since Victor and Detective West worked together on his last case with CID, he dropped by the club every once in a while. He would often pick Victor's brain on certain cases.

Thirty minutes later, he strolled through the glass door. The place was in chaos. Being in this type of atmosphere again brought back memories. He spotted Detective West arguing with a young man in handcuffs.

"Tell me who sold you the stolen goods, then we can talk," Detective West yelled. The man refused to talk. He glanced over the man's shoulder and spotted Victor. "Put him in a cell until he finds his memory," he instructed an officer.

Victor smiled and shook his head. "Still laying down the law, I see."

"What the hell are you doing here, or do I know?"

"You know," Victor answered.

Detective West pointed at Victor. "The Dani McCall case." He led him into his office, and then closed the door behind them.

"Tonya hired me to do some investigative work," Victor said.

"Investigative work?" Detective West asked in surprise. "I thought you gave that up."

"I did," Victor answered. "But then I decided to open my own investigative agency."

Detective West leaned back. "Your own investigative agency. Do you have a license?"

"Not yet." He arched a knowing eyebrow. "That's where you come in."

Detective West chuckled. "That's where I come in?" he repeated. "How so?"

"You can cut through the red tape for me after I register with the state," Victor said. "Since I'm already on a case, you can push it through for me."

"I can do that, but what's in it for me?" Detective West asked. He had been after Victor to speak to the Cadets at the Police Academy.

"What if I finally agree to speak to the Cadets at the Academy?"

"That's a start," Detective West said. "You have a stellar law enforcement career. I know you won't have a problem getting the license to open your agency or carry a concealed weapon. I'm sure you can pass the background check," he said with a slow drawl.

"A start?" Victor questioned. "Why don't you just spit it out? What else do you want from me?"

Detective West smiled. "I want you to work with us on some cases."

Victor's head snapped up. "The Police Department?"

Detective West walked behind his desk and sat down. "Work with us or forget about the license."

Victor chuckled. "You cannot stop me from getting the license."

"Maybe not, but I can hold up the process for quite a while." Detective West opened the file on his desk. "You won't be able to help attorney Sims."

Victor opened his mouth to speak.

"Legally," Detective West added.

"You wouldn't?" Victor asked in surprise.

"I get it. You want to be your own boss," Detective West explained. "You want to work with private clients, but we would like your expertise. Come on, what do you say?"

"Haven't I been working for you?" Victor asked. "What about the advice I was giving you on some cases?"

"Well, now you will get paid for your services."

"And we will be formally working together?" Victor asked.

"Yes. I think it could be a win, win situation."

"I admit it can work out for both of us," Victor agreed.

"Now that we have that out of the way, what can I do for you?" Detective West asked.

"I would like to see the body," Victor explained.

"I can do that," Detective West said, heading for the door. "Let's take a walk downstairs. Have you looked at the crime scene?"

"I just came from there," Victor said, falling in step with Detective West. "You better speak with Mrs. Sterling. She crossed the crime scene."

"That woman is a pain in the you know what. I told her that we would let her know when she could go back to the mansion," Detective West said.

"I guess she couldn't wait," Victor said.

"We're sending someone out to speak with her," Detective West said. "What do you think about the crime scene?"

"It was a professional hit," Victor said. "It was two simultaneous clean shots from about twenty yards and through the curtains. No way was it an amateur."

"That's what I thought, too," Detective West said. "Any leads on who hired him?"

"How do you know it's a he?" Victor said. "Could have been a she."

Detective West gave Victor a look. "Never thought of that."

"Anyway, I'm just getting started," Victor said.

"My money is still on Dani McCall," Detective West said. "She had a motive after he fired her."

"He didn't fire her. She was suspended," Victor said. "He did fire Jimmy Parker and Ginger Fox. They could have also done it."

"True. But their alibis check out," Detective West said. "Dani McCall's doesn't. The murder weapon was found in her car."

"What about ballistics?" Victor asked.

"Nothing back yet," Detective West said. "We still haven't found anyone that saw her in a bar on the night of the murder. I'm sure attorney Sims showed you the report."

"But remember it looks like a professional hit," Victor said. "Which means that the killer was hired."

"Which could have been your new client," Detective West said.

"I'll admit it looks bad," Victor said.

"That's an understatement," Detective West said. "I don't want to see you lose your first case."

"Who says that I'm going to lose it?" Victor asked.

"I just spelled it out for you," Detective West said. "The odds are stacked against you and attorney Sims."

"Just the way we like it. Is Lucia still around?" he said, changing the subject.

"Where is she going?" Detective West asked. "She's been there for over twenty years. She knows everything and everybody. Not to mention she's the best Medical Examiner in the tri-state area."

"And loves to talk nonstop." Victor chuckled, following Detective West through the thick, iron doors. "I cannot argue about her skills."

The cold air hit Victor in the face. It was freezing. He looked around to see several employees working on bodies.

Lucia looked up when they strolled in. A slow smile crossed her face. "As I live and breathe. I don't believe it." She hurried over and threw her arms around Victor's neck. "What a surprise."

"Hello, Lucia." Victor smiled. "How are you?"

"I'm great, Colonel. What about you?"

"I'm fine."

"How's that lovely Dominique?"

"Still lovely," Victor answered.

"What are you doing here?" Lucia continued.

"He's here to take a look at Mr. Sterling's body," Detective West answered for him.

"Are you investigating again?" Lucia asked.

"Yes, I am," Victor answered.

"I'm not surprised," Lucia said. "Men like you are born to investigate. I was wondering how long it was going to take you to leave that club."

"You sound like Dominique."

Lucia shrugged. "Truth is truth."

"He's even opened his own agency," Detective West boasted.

"Good for you," Lucia said. "That means we may see a lot more of you around here. Anything I can do to help, just let me know."

"I will hold you to that," Victor said. "What can you tell me about Montgomery Sterling?"

"Poor guy," Lucia said. "Never stood a chance." She walked over and pulled opened the cold chamber that the victim laid in.

"From what I could tell, he was shot from about twenty yards away. It looks professional to me," Victor said, examining the body.

"That's what we figure as well," Detective West said.

"Both of your analogies would be correct," Lucia said.

"He was killed with a .357 Desert Eagle Automatic?" Victor said.

"You get the prize," Lucia said. "The first shot killed him. He was dead before he hit the floor."

"Ouch!" Victor exclaimed. "What about the time of death? The report I read says between nine and eleven p.m. Has it changed?"

"The findings haven't changed," Lucia said.

"The murder weapon that was found in Dani McCall's car is the one that killed Montgomery Sterling," Detective West said. "She has no alibi for the time of the killing. She's the killer. Case closed."

***

"Three hundred and fifty-thousand-dollars?" Dani said, trailing Tonya into the club office. "I had to put my house up for collateral. The D.A. is asking for life in prison."

"At least you're out of jail," Tonya said.

"There is no way I can spend the rest of my life behind bars," Dani said. "I just can't."

"Don't worry about that now. Have a seat." Tonya walked around and plopped down in Gerald's chair. "We can talk here a moment."

"This is like a nightmare. I want to thank you again for taking my case" Dani said. "You have been like a rock to me. I'm not surprise, even in college you were the most reliable out of the group."

"I don't know about that," Tonya said. "There's no need to thank me. You needed my help. I was able to give it."

"I saw Victor in court this morning," Dani said. "Gerald picked me up from the station. Your family is really going all out for me."

"Victor has already began working on the case. We went out to see the crime scene and spoke with Mrs. Sterling. He's very good at what he does. If anyone can get at the truth of what happened, he can."

Dani sat up straight. "What have you found out so far?"

"Well, it's still early," Tonya said. "Victor still needs to speak with Jimmy Farmer and Ginger Fox. But it looks like Mr. Sterling was killed by a professional."

"What?" Dani asked. "A professional killer?"

Tonya nodded.

Dani shook her head. "That's not good. It means that even if I have an alibi I could have hired someone to do it for me."

"That's how it looks," Tonya said. "But it would help a lot if you have one."

"What I know for certain is I began drinking early that day. I know it started at Cadence." Dani ran a hand through her hair in frustration. "I don't remember what time I left."

"We have cameras installed throughout the club," Tonya said. "We can look at the video."

"That will help me a lot," Dani said. "I am not a drinker." She shook her head. "What did you find out about Mrs. Sterling?"

"She's not grieving over his death," Tonya said.

"Not too many people will be," Dani said. "He was a terrible man."

"So I've heard. Look, now that you are out on bail, I would like to set some ground rules."

"Ground rules?" Dani exclaimed. "I am too old for ground rules."

"If you want me to continue representing you, you will follow my rules."

"Don't worry, she will follow any rules you set," Maya said, hurrying into the office. She rushed over and threw her arm around Dani's neck. "Sister, it is good to have you home."

"It's good to be home," Dani said.

Maya stepped back. "Are you alright? Did they hurt you?"

"I wasn't hurt," Dani said. "That place is horrible. The sooner we get the trial over with, the better."

"What the prosecution has so far is circumstantial," Tonya said.

"So, we can refute it?" Dani inquired.

"With what we have so far. Yes," Tonya said. "Hopefully, nothing will come up before the pretrial."

"You have to prove my innocence at the preliminary trial," Dani pleaded. "I don't want to stand trial for something that I didn't do."

"That's the plan," Tonya said.

"When is the preliminary trial?" Maya asked.

"I don't have a date yet," Tonya said. "I hope to get a date as soon as possible."

"I don't know how we will ever repay you," Maya said.

"As I told Dani," Tonya said, "I'm glad to be able to help. Now for those ground rules. I want you to look and act confident, look healthy, and get plenty of rest. Under no circumstances do I want you to drink alcohol, have visitors, go out, and absolutely do not speak to the press. Is that clear?"

"Maybe I should go back to jail?" Dani said sarcastically.

"I can arrange that if you want," Tonya said. "Any questions?"

Dani sighed. "Yeah, if I can't go out, how do I get personal things done?"

"Maya can get you anything that you need," Tonya suggested.

Dani glanced at Maya. "I guess you will be taking care of me for a change."

"Looks like it," Maya quipped.

***

Victor got off on the sixth floor of WADC News. The staff were running around like chickens with their heads cut off. He grabbed a hold of a young girl rushing past him. "I'm looking for Ginger Fox. I was told that she would be here."

The young lady pointed. "Through those doors," she said and hurried off.

Victor walked down the tile hallway. He pushed the doors open and found himself in the middle of live news broadcast.

"No one is allowed back here," a man said, walking up to block Victor.

"My name is Victor Sexton. I'm working with Dani McCall's attorney. I was told by Ms. Fox that I could meet her here."

The man drew his eyebrows together. "Sexton? You're Victor Sexton?"

Victor leaned back. "Have we met?"

"No," the man said. "I know a lot about you." He extended a hand to Victor. "I'm Alston Albright. I'm Ms. Fox's attorney. She is just wrapping up. How is Dani?"

"Under the circumstances, she is holding up well."

"I'm happy to hear that," Alston said. "She is a good woman and a great reporter."

"From what I know about her, I would have to agree," Victor said. "I thought Ms. Fox was fired."

"She was. The son rehired her. It's not the main anchor, but she is working and that's all that matters."

"That was kind of sudden, wasn't it?" Victor asked. "Mr. Sterling hasn't even been buried yet and Ms. Fox is already back at work."

"You mean it makes her looks guilty," Alston said. "Gives her a motive."

"I'm sure you know that Ms. Fox is already a suspect."

"If she wasn't, you would not be here, Mr. Sexton."

"True."

"My client didn't kill Mr. Sterling, Mr. Sexton. As far as her being back at work, she never should have been fired in the first place."

Victor glanced to see Ginger Fox heading in his direction. She was still as beautiful as she was when she first appeared on the air fifteen years ago.

"You must be Victor Sexton." A smile spread across Ginger's face. She extended a petite hand.

"I am." Victor accepted it. He turned it over and planted a kiss on the back of it.

"Charming," Ginger said. "I like that. What can I do for you?"

"He's working for Dani McCall's attorney," Alston quipped.

"Of course, he is," Ginger said. "Alston give us a minute. I will meet you downstairs."

Alston gave Victor a look before finally leaving them alone.

"Don't mind him," Ginger said. "He's harmless."

"Good to know."

"I don't think for a second that Dani killed Montgomery," Ginger said. "I will tell you everything that I know to help her. Let's walk and talk."

"Thank you." Victor fell in step with Ginger. "First, let me say that I am a huge fan of yours. Whenever I could, I never missed any of your broadcasts."

Ginger's face beamed. "Thanks."

"How well did you know Montgomery Sterling?"

"Not only did I work for Mr. Montgomery, but we also did some Women Rights work together," Ginger said. "Mainly fundraising."

"I remember hearing about that," Victor said. "I read that you are really into The Women Rights Movement."

"I was," Ginger said.

"What happened?"

"It became too much," she said. "I was working here and doing the fundraising. It became too much for me."

"How did Mr. Sterling feel about that?" Victor asked. "From what I know about his nature, he doesn't take too kindly to people quitting on him. Women Rights is a big issue in this country. Being involved in something like that not only brought in millions for the cause, it made the company and Mr. Sterling look good to be involved."

"Everything you said is true," Ginger said.

"Then you had a contract with him?"

"Right again."

"Did breaking the contract have something to do with you being fired?" Victor asked.

"Look, I thought you came here to talk to me about getting Dani off," Ginger said. "Why all of the questions about me?"

"You know that I have to ask you these questions to find out who really killed Montgomery Sterling."

"No matter how I felt about Mr. Sterling, I did not kill him. You see, I was at another fundraiser event for cancer research," she said with pleasure. "Four hundred people can vouch for me. Women Rights is not the only cause that I raise money for. Satisfied?"

"It looks like the killer was a hired gun," Victor said.

"What does that have to do with me?"

"He did fire you," Victor said.

"He was going to rehire me," Ginger said.

"What made you think that he was going to keep his word?"

"Trust me. He would have rehired me," Ginger said. "Now if you will excuse me, I need to get back to work."

"We will speak again."

"You know where to find me," Ginger said over her right shoulder as she walked away.

Victor made his way to his truck. As he opened the door, his cell phone rang. He recognized the number belonging to Jimmy Farmer. He had been trying to get in contact with him all morning. "Hello, Mr. Farmer. Nice of you to call me back."

"Yeah. Yeah. What can I do for you?"

"I need to speak with you," Victor said.

"What is this about?"

"It's about the murder of Montgomery Sterling."

The line went silent.

"Mr. Farmer?" Victor prompted.

"What makes you think that I know anything about that?"

"That's why I need to speak with you," Victor said. "Where can I meet you, Mr. Farmer?"

"Okay. My address is 5501 Saddleback Road, Washington, D.C. It's the Boys Club."

"I'm not too far away. I know exactly where it is," Victor said. "I will be there shortly."

"I will wait for you outside. I don't want anyone to know that I'm speaking with you."

Ten minutes later, Victor pulled up in front of the Boys Club. He didn't notice anyone standing out front. It was eerily quiet. Maybe Mr. Farmer was busy. He got out of the truck and headed inside the building.

Victor stepped in the waiting area. He found no one at the front desk. He past the reception area and peeped in the first open door on the left. He spotted a man with his back to him.

"Excuse me," Victor called. "I'm looking for Jimmy Farmer. I was supposed to meet him out front, but no one was there." He strolled further into the room. The man appeared to be going through folders on the desk.

"I haven't seen anyone," the man said. "I'm just here to empty the trash cans."

Victor glanced at the can next to the desk. It was full. The floor needed to be vacuumed. He noticed that the man was not dressed in a janitorial uniform but street clothes, and there was no cart outside the door.

"Well, looks like you have your work cut out for you today."

"This place is always dirty," the man said. His back was still to Victor.

"Always busy here, huh?"

"Always," he said.

"Don't you think you should be getting back to work?" Victor asked. "The trash cans need to be emptied and the floor could use a vacuum."

"I'm done for the day," the man said over his right shoulder.

"Who are you guys?" a woman asked, appearing out of nowhere. "What are you doing in here?"

The man took the opportunity to rush out past them, knocking the woman over.

"Wait a minute," Victor called after him. He disappeared out the door before he could get a good look at him. He refocused on the woman. "Are you alright?"

"I'm fine," the woman said as Victor helped her to her feet. "Who was he?"

"I don't know," Victor replied. "I found him in the office. He told me that he was the janitor."

"Our janitor's name is Rosa," the woman said. "She's been with us for about five years."

"I was supposed to meet Mr. Farmer out front," Victor said.

"Mr. Farmer is gone for the day," the woman said.

"When did he leave?" Victor asked.

"About ten minutes ago," she said. "He took a phone call and left right after that."

"How long has Mr. Farmer been working here?"

"He's been volunteering here about ten years." She looked inquisitively at Victor and asked. "Who are you?"

"I work for the attorney that is representing Dani McCall."

"The lady accused of killing the owner of the news station?"

"That's the one," Victor said. "And you are?"

"I'm Cassie Stringer. I'm the receptionist. You think Mr. Farmer knows something about the murder?" Cassie said. "Or maybe killed him?"

"Or had him killed," Victor said.

"Look, Mr. Farmer is a good man," Cassie said. "He is the reason why the Boys Club is still open. Do you know what that means to this community? No one who has done so much for these boys would kill someone. He didn't do it."

"Do you know that for sure?" Victor asked. "Can you give him an alibi?"

"If I have too," Cassie said. "I will."

Chapter Six

"The cocktail hour centerpiece is perfect," Dominique said. "You really outdid yourself." She traced her fingers along the red, burgundy, and fuchsia flowers. The arrangement included black magic roses, hydrangeas, Vanda orchids, and tall red gloriosa lilies situated in bamboo and lanterns.

"Thank you. I hope Meghan likes it," Valencia Hill, the wedding planner said. "I really love the candle in the middle. I think it adds a special ambiance to the event, placed on each table."

Dominique smiled at her warmly. "You really have an eye for detail. When the time come, you will plan my wedding."

"You bet I will."

The bell over the door caused Dominique and Valencia to glance around to Tonya coming through it.

"Hey, girl." Dominique leaned over, giving her a hug. "You're the last person I expected to see. Where are you coming from?"

"Home," Tonya said. "I was on my way to grab something to eat when I saw you."

"Where's your client?"

Tonya removed her shades. "She's home. I banished her there."

Valencia chuckled. "My next appointment is here. I'll talk to you guys later." She strolled over to help a client.

"Where are you headed?" Dominique asked. "I'm starving."

"I only had yogurt this morning. I'm dying for something to eat."

Just as they turned to leave, Tonya's cell phone rang. It was Victor. She prayed that he had some good news. "It's Victor. Hello." She listened intently for a moment. "So, Farmer wasn't there? What is the chance of him returning? Fifty-Fifty?" Tonya looked to see her cousin, Paul, passing the shop. "You need someone to watch the Boys Club, right? I think I may have found someone. I will call you back." She ended the call.

"Victor didn't want to speak to me?" Dominique asked.

Tonya ignored her. Paul was looking straight ahead. She knocked on the glass window to get his attention. She hurried outside to catch him. Grabbing his arm, she hustled him inside the bridal shop. A bewildered look crossed his face.

Paul leaned back. "Could your smile be any bigger? What the hell is going on?"

"Some surveillance work," Tonya said in an excited voice.

"Surveillance work?" Paul asked. "What are you talking about? Did someone forget to pay their taxes or something?"

"No. This is a criminal case."

Paul's eyes stretched. "Since when are you handling criminal cases?"

"Since I began representing Dani McCall."

"What? Wait?" Paul said. "You are representing Dani McCall? The anchorwoman charged with killing her boss?"

"I don't have time to explain that part right now," Tonya said. "There is a man named Jimmy Farmer—"

"The news anchor that was fired a couple of weeks back," Paul interrupted.

"Right. Victor was to meet him at the Boys Club where he volunteers, but he left before Victor got there."

"Victor is also on the case?" Paul asked in surprise.

"Paul focus," Tonya scolded. "This is important. I just need you to watch the Boys Club to see if Mr. Farmer will return. Victor is watching his home, and so far, he hasn't shown up there either. Can you do it?"

"You know I was Special Ops like Victor," Paul reminded her. "I think I can handle a surveillance gig."

Tonya's face dropped. "I'm sorry. I know you can. It's just that I haven't handled a criminal case in a long time. I'm anxious. This one is special. Nothing can go wrong."

Paul removed the car keys out of his pocket. "Text me the address? I'll call Victor and have him fill me in."

"Sure," Tonya said. She took out her phone, her fingers expertly flying over the keys. She quickly sent Paul the address and a picture of Jimmy Farmer she found on social media.

"Will you be taking on more criminal cases?" Paul asked. "Or is this a one-time thing?"

"I don't know. Victor is opening his own investigative agency. It is called VSI. I took a leave of absence to take on this case."

"Tonya!" Dominque squealed. "You did? Will you go back after the case is over?"

"I don't know," Tonya answered. "That depends on Victor."

Dominique smiled. "I was telling Victor it would be great if you two worked together. You do the legal work and he does the investigating."

"I like that idea," Tonya said.

"Will you need more investigators?" Paul asked.

"I'm sure that he will, and you are family," Dominique said. "You already have your first assignment."

"Speaking of which," Paul said. "I better get going." With a wave of a hand, he rushed out the door.

"That was nice of you," Dominique said.

"What?"

"Involving Paul," Dominique answered. "You know he's had a tough time since he got out of the army."

Together they stepped out into the sunshine. Tonya replaced her sunglasses. "Everything has to go well. There are a lot of people depending on the outcome of this case."

"I know that it will," Dominique said. "I will do my part to make sure that VSI is successful. I believe this is fate. Look at what happened and how it happened. I'm not saying Victor wasn't happy at Cadence, but this is more of who he is. Let's head over to Lizano's," she suggested. "It's only a block away."

"Sounds good," Tonya agreed. "Criminal law is more of who I am."

They began walking along the bustling sidewalk. People could be seen entering and exiting the shops with bags in hand. It was a warm May afternoon in Washington, D.C. Blue skies stretched as far as the eyes could see. The temperature was in the mid-eighties. It was a good day to have lunch outside. Once they arrived at the café, they were quickly escorted to a table beneath a red and white striped tapestry.

"Victor was telling me that you were once a criminal lawyer," Dominique said. "I didn't know that. Why you never said anything?"

The waiter handed both women a menu. He placed a basket of chips and dip on the table.

Tonya flashed a weak smile. "It's true. I graduated top of my class at Harvard Law. I practiced for five years. I met Stephen. We fell in love. He didn't want to be married to a criminal attorney. I gave it up to become a tax attorney."

"Wow," Dominque said. "Just like that?"

"I can understand your response," Tonya said in amazement. "Not many women these days would have given up what I gave up."

"I don't know. I guess that depends on the woman," Dominique said. "Was it worth it?"

"Sometimes yes. Sometimes no," Tonya said.

"I mean I can see his point, sometimes being a criminal lawyer can be dangerous. You're representing all types of people accused of doing all kinds of things. Do you miss it?"

"Sometimes."

"I feel like I have had this conversation with another member of your family," Dominique said with a smile.

"My brother."

"I think you two are more alike than you think," Dominique said. She opened the menu.

"I think so, too."

"Are you happy doing tax law, Tonya?" Dominique asked.

Tonya was quiet a moment. "No," she finally answered.

"Have you spoken to Stephen about it?"

Tonya shook her head.

"Why not?"

"Because when we got married, he told me what type of wife he wanted. One that could work as long as she was home to cook dinner and be a mother to his kids," Tonya explained. "I agreed to that because I loved him and thought it was what I wanted at the time."

"And now?"

"I miss being a criminal attorney. I felt it at first," Tonya said, "then when this case came along…"

"You knew for certain," Dominique finished for her.

"Yes," Tonya said. "And now I get the chance to work with my brother. I'm on cloud nine."

"How are you going to work with Victor?"

Tonya shrugged. "I don't know. I love my husband, but I'm not happy doing tax law. One day, I'm going to have to tell him the truth."

Dominique reached out and covered Tonya's hand with hers. "Maybe you guys can work something out."

"I hope so," Tonya said. "I don't want to lose my family, but I no longer want to ignore who I really am."

"I understand," Dominique said. "I pray that Stephen does as well."

"So do I," Tonya agreed.

Dominique took her time scanning the menu before deciding upon a chicken salad and a diet Pepsi. Tonya ordered the same.

Tonya munched on a chip. "Have you heard from your aunt and uncle? I know how close you are to them," she asked, changing the subject.

"No. I can understand Uncle Harold not talking to me," Dominique scowled, "but not Aunt Rosetta."

"Do you regret choosing my brother over your family?"

"No," Dominique answered without hesitation.

The ping of the cell phone interrupted the conversation. Dominique checked. She received several photos from Victor. She clicked on the pictures. Victor's smiling face jumped out at her. The caption read: *Future Home of VSI.*

"Nice," Dominique said, scrolling through the photos. "I already see how I can decorate."

Tonya leaned across the table. "I claim that office."

***

"Welcome to the team," Victor said in the phone to Paul. He was parked outside Jimmy Farmer's home. There was still no sign of him.

"Thank you," Paul said. "Great to be aboard. I just arrived at the Boy's Club. No one is

around. Lights out. The place looks empty." He read the sign on the front door. Open from

from 9 a.m. to 7 p.m. He glanced at his watch. It was 7:30. "According to the sign on the door, they closed thirty minutes ago. What's happening on your end?" Paul asked.

"Same here," Victor said. "No sign of Mr. Farmer. Keep your eyes open. Earlier, I ran into a shady character. He got away from me. He could also be hanging around waiting for Farmer to show."

"Got it," Paul said. "How long should I wait?"

"Give it another hour or two," Victor instructed. "If no one shows up…" His voice trailed off when he spotted Jimmy Farmer drive up in a white BMW. "Our boy just showed up. I'm texting you the address. Make your way over here but wait outside."

"I'm on my way," Paul said.

As Victor was about to exit the truck, a Lexus pulled up behind Farmer. A man that appeared to be in his late thirties or early forties got out. He rushed over to Farmer. The two men got into a heated argument. He could not make out what was being said. Farmer suddenly turned and hurried inside the house. The other man followed. He looked familiar. Victor reached for the folder on the front seat and flipped through the photos until he came to his picture. Spencer Sterling, the son of Montgomery Sterling. *What were they arguing about? Was he going to rehire Jimmy Farmer like he did Ginger?* There was only one way to find out. He got out the truck and walked up to the door.

Victor could hear loud voices on the outside. "I said no!" Jimmy was saying. "That's it! We have nothing else to discuss. Spencer, please leave!"

"We're not finished talking," Spencer said.

"Yes, we are!"

Victor could hear a scuffle in progress. He rang the doorbell. The movement ceased. The next sound was footsteps moving toward the door. The door swung open. He was face-to-face with Spencer Sterling.

"Yes?" Spencer said. "What can I do for you?"

"My name is Victor Sexton."

"And?"

"And I'm working for the attorney on the Dani McCall's case." Victor noticed Spencer's mouth gaped a little. "I have an appointment to see Jimmy Farmer."

"Come on in, Mr. Sexton," Jimmy said. His face was beet red. He appeared agitated. "I'm sorry that I could not wait for you earlier. I had to leave. I'm sorry about that."

"I better get going," Spencer said. He rushed outside.

"You don't have to run off, Mr. Sterling," Victor said hot on his trail.

The coloring drained from Spencer's face. "You know who I am?"

"It's my business to know," Victor answered. "I'm sorry about your father. If you don't mind, I have a few questions."

Spencer composed himself. "Why would I mind?"

"Good. Were you and your father close?"

"My mother died when I was fifteen. After her death all we had were each other."

"But he sent you away to school."

Spencer dropped his head. "Yes, that's right. Military boarding school. It turned out to be good for me. I learned discipline there first, and then in college. But we spent summers and holidays together."

"Sounds like a charming life," Victor said.

"Mr. Sexton, my father was a difficult man. It was not easy being his son."

"What about working for him?"

"That was even harder," Spencer answered in a flat tone.

"You don't have to worry about that anymore," Victor said. "All of his wealth, position, and power are yours now."

"Eventually it would have been mine anyway," Spencer said. "He was grooming me to take over."

"I heard a different story," Victor said. "I heard that your father barely paid you what he paid his secretary. He gave you no authority, even though you were in charge. It was all for show. He knew that you were afraid to leave your position but didn't really want to stay."

"I know one thing for sure, Mr. Sexton. I'm not afraid of you." Spencer sidestepped Victor. He strolled toward the car and said over his right shoulder, "Dani is guilty. She's going to pay for killing my father."

"What makes you believe that she is guilty?" Victor asked. "What is her motive?"

A smirk appeared on Spencer's face. "My father placed her on administrative leave without pay for a week," he said. "He placed her assistant, Marissa Prentiss, in her anchor chair."

"I know that," Victor said.

"Well did you know she announced to a room full of people, including me, that she was going to kill him. Next thing I know, my father is dead. That is not a coincidence." Without another word, Spencer opened the door of his vehicle and drove away.

Victor could imagine him grinning from ear-to-ear all the way down the street.

. He turned to find Mr. Farmer standing in the door with both hands stuffed in his pockets.

"He's a real piece of work, isn't he?" He walked outside to speak with Victor.

"Yes, he is," Victor said. "What were you two arguing about?"

"Nothing that concerns you."

"Let me be the judge of that," Victor said.

"I told you on the phone that I don't know anything about Mr. Sterling's murder."

"Didn't you see him the night he died?"

Jimmy blinked. "You must have spoken to the police."

"I read the report," Victor said. "Now tell me the real reason why you met him on the night he died."

"I saw him at E Street Club," Jimmy admitted. "I bought him a drink."

"Why would you do that after he fired you?" Victor asked.

"Because he called me to tell me that he was going to give me my job back," Jimmy said. "We both like Jazz. He invited me to E Street Club to smooth things over and make amends. I would have done anything to get my job back."

"Including kill him?"

"Why would I do that when I just told you that he was going to give me my job back?" Jimmy said. "I just told you we were together at the club."

"He left an hour before you did," Victor said.

"I stayed at the club," Jimmy said. "A lot of people saw me there. I didn't leave until the club closed. I have witnesses."

"It won't wash, Jimmy."

"What? Why?" Jimmy asked. "I didn't kill him."

"You see," Victor said. "The killer hired a professional to do his dirty work."

"A professional?" Jimmy repeated.

"So, it doesn't matter who saw you at the club," Victor pointed out. "You could have easily hired someone to do it for you."

"But I didn't," Jimmy said.

"We will see, won't we?" Victor said. Without another word, he walked toward Paul who just drove up.

"Jimmy Farmer?" Paul asked.

"Yes."

"We have more problems?" Paul said.

"We do? How?"

"Someone on the street just gave me this." Paul handed Victor a flyer.

"Twenty-five-thousand-dollars reward for information revealing seller or purchase of a Sterling murder gun, 357 Desert Eagle Automatic. Serial Number filed, cracked handle, and silencer," Victor read aloud. He was flabbergasted. "You have got to be kidding me. Who did you get this from?"

"The young man that handed it to me said Maya McCall paid him to give them out," Paul answered. "I took the stack from him, gave him a fifty-dollar bill, and sent him home."

"I don't believe this," Victor said. "Let's go."

***

"These were plastered and handed out all over D.C.," Victor said, storming into Cadence. "What the hell is going on?"

"This one was given to me by someone on the street," Tonya said.

"And you didn't tell me?" Victor snapped.

"I have been passing them out," Maya announced proud of herself. "I gave some fellow students a couple of dollars to help me out. I think it is straight forward. I wanted to appeal to anyone that had information about the gun."

Victor rubbed a hand across his forehead. He didn't like stupidity and was doing his best to control his anger. "This is…"

Tonya shook her head for him to take it easy.

"I do not have the words," Victor said.

"Thanks," Maya beamed.

"I don't think that is what he wanted to say," Tonya said. "Maya, what you have done is—"

"Dangerous," Victor finished for his sister. "Reckless. Stupid."

"Victor," Tonya scolded.

"You could be hurt. Who put this ridiculous idea in your head? Was it your sister?" Victor shouted.

"It was the right thing to do," Maya said. "I wanted to help."

"Maya," Victor began. "No, it wasn't."

"A lot of people will read it," Maya continued. "Like Dani said, we can get some great leads that will prove that she did not kill Mr. Sterling."

"You left your cell number?" Paul asked.

"Well, yeah," Maya said. "I want people to call me. It's not like I left my home address or anything. Just my phone number." She shrugged. "Who would hurt me? They want the money."

"How about the real killer?" Victor asked.

Maya's face dropped. "Oh my God. I didn't think about that."

Victor shook his head in disbelief.

"What are we going to do?" Paul asked. "These are all over the city."

"Well, we will have to get someone to stay close to her and Dani."

"No thank you," Maya said. "We will be just fine."

"Someone should be watching the house," Victor argued.

"Not until I discuss it with Dani," Maya argued. "She already feels cooped up."

"I'll have a talk with Dani. Where is she?" Victor asked.

"She's being bedazzled by Gerald in the office," Tonya replied.

"How are you going to know if the caller is for real?" Paul asked.

"That's easy," Maya said with confidence. "I left out the part about the handle being white and has a picture of a skull and cross bone on it. Only the person that sold or know about the weapon will know that."

Paul leaned his head to one side. "That's good thinking."

"But it was still a stupid thing to do." Victor took off toward the back of the club.

"Is there something else I need to know?" Tonya called after him.

"Paul will feel you in," Victor called over his right shoulder.

"He's mad at me," Maya said as she watched Victor disappear around the corner.

"Yep," Paul said. "He sure is."

***

"Abbey left here about an hour ago," Devin Torres of Clint's Pawn Shop said to the man. "She ran out the door."

"Where did she go?" Priest asked.

"I don't know," Devin said. "All I know is that she was really excited about something. She acted like she won the lottery or something."

"Reward money." Priest picked up the flyer off the glass case.

"Lots of money," Devin said. "One minutes she was reading that flyer. The next minute she was gone. It made me think that she must know something about the Sterling murder case."

Priest spit out his gum onto the flyer and headed toward the door.

"Listen, tell Abbey if she gets that cash, that I deserve half of it," Devin said. "I was the one that brought the flyer to her attention."

"I'll make sure to tell her," Priest said on his way out the door.

***

"I don't need police protection," Dani said. "I refuse."

"We know about the flyers," Victor said.

"Maya was only helping me out," Dani said.

"It was a stupid thing to do," Victor exclaimed.

"You cannot talk to me like that," Dani said.

"I just did," Victor countered. "Look, you hired us to prove that you are innocent. We cannot do our job effectively if we get distracted by stupid stunts."

"First you removed the alcohol from my house, took my car keys, and now you are treating me like a child. I don't need a babysitter. I'm already about to go stir crazy."

"That should be the least of your worries," Victor countered.

"What are you babbling about?" Dani inquired.

"Why didn't you tell us that you threatened to kill Montgomery Sterling?"

"What?" Tonya exclaimed, coming into Gerald's office.

"Are you serious?" Gerald threw in. "That doesn't mean—"

Victor shooed everyone in the room. "I was talking to Dani."

"You don't have to be rude," Gerald said, quietly going back to sit behind his desk.

"What about it Dani?" Victor repeated. "Did you threaten to kill him?"

"Who told you that?" Dani asked. "Spencer Sterling?"

Maya let out a soft gasp. "Dani?"

"Then it is true?" Victor asked.

Dani panicked. "Look, I spoke out of anger. I didn't mean it."

"He put your assistant in your anchor chair. You then announced that you wanted to kill him in front of a room full of people, but you didn't mean it. Is that your story?"

"He suspended me without pay," Dani explained. "Does it look bad?" she asked.

Tonya chuckled. "Does it look bad? What do you think?"

"So that is what happened?" Maya said. "That's why you didn't go on air that day. You told me that you were on vacation."

"You told me the same lie," Tonya said.

"I know how bad it looks," Dani said.

"Do you?" Tonya said.

"That's why I didn't want to say anything."

"Didn't want to say anything?" Tonya echoed. "I'm your attorney. You can lie to other people but not to me."

"Not to us," Victor corrected.

"We are the ones sticking our neck out for you," Tonya said. "What if I were to go into court and was suddenly blindsided by this news. You need to be totally honest with us."

Dani didn't respond.

"If I found out about it, I can guarantee you that the prosecution will find out about it, too," Victor said.

"I hear what you are saying," Dani said. "But I still didn't kill him. Didn't you tell me that it was a professional killer?"

"That's what the evidence is pointing to," Victor said. "That's what makes putting out the flyers even more dangerous."

"No more lies, Dani. Or I am walking," Tonya threatened.

"No more lies," Dani agreed.

"What about police protection?" Victor asked.

"No," Dani answered. "No police protection. We will be fine."

"I don't like the idea of you going back to your place alone," Victor said.

"What about your place in Maryland?" Gerald asked. "You don't stay there often. Maybe she can stay there until things cool down."

Victor pointed at Gerald. "Brother, you are always thinking. I think that's a great idea. You can be their bodyguard."

"Gerald?" the room asked in unison.

Gerald's eyes stretched. "Me? A bodyguard? You must be kidding. I'm a club owner. I don't know anything about police or detective work or whatever you want to call it."

"But you know about watching women, which is what you will be doing," Victor said, stroking his brother's ego. "You are good at that."

"What if the killer shows up?" Gerald asked. "What do I do then?"

"Don't worry, I will protect you," Dani joked.

Gerald made a face. "Funny."

Dani frowned. "Where is your place?"

"In Gaithersburg," Victor answered.

"You don't live there?" Dani asked.

"Not often," Victor answered.

"He spends a lot of his time at his fiancée's place," Tonya said.

"Okay, let's get going," Victor instructed.

"I need to stop by my place to pick up some things," Dani said.

"I'll go instead," Maya said. "Just head over to Victor's place."

"Good idea. Gerald and Tonya will go with Dani," Victor instructed. "Maya will drop by their place for Dani."

"You're not coming?" Dani asked.

"I need to go over surveillance videos from the club," Victor answered. "Paul, you are with me."

Chapter Seven

Maya turned the key in the lock and let herself inside the house she and Dani share together. She made her way into the living room, placing her large bag on the sofa. She quickly rambled around in it to find the phone. She glanced at it to find that she already had over fifty messages. Excited, she went through them one by one, until one from a young lady by the name of Abbey Knowles gave her the information that she was looking for. The cracked handle was white with a picture of a cross bone and skull on it. She insisted that Maya call her back. She had to let Victor know at once. This could be the break in the case that could help her sister, then he wouldn't be so angry at her.

A loud rap caused Maya to jump. "Yes!" she called, pressing the intercom button.

"I'm here about the flyer." the male voice answered.

"How did you find me?" Maya yelled at the door. "I didn't list my address."

A moment later, her cell phone on the kitchen counter vibrated.

"One second please, my phone is ringing." Maya strolled over to the counter. She recognized the number. It was her sister, Dani. "Hi, sis."

"Maya?" Dani called. "How long will you be?"

"I won't be long?"

"I don't like you being there alone."

"I'm fine," Maya said. "If anything happens, I will dial 911. Someone by the name of Abbey Knowles left me a voicemail. She said she may have sold the .357 Desert

Eagle Automatic to the killer. She knows about the white handle and the artwork on it. She wants to meet at the Old Fisherman's Wharf at five o'clock. On top of that, there is a man at the door asking about the flyer."

"Don't do anything until you speak to Victor," Dani said. "Wait a second, you didn't put the address on the flyer, did you?"

"No. I did not."

"How did he find you?"

"I don't know," Maya said. "I plan on asking him."

"Do not open the door!" Dani yelled. "Call the police. I'm going to call Victor and tell him what is going on."

"What do you want me to do?" Maya asked. "He's already here at the door."

"Stall," Dani instructed. "But do not open the door."

"I want to see what he knows," Maya said.

"I mean it, Maya!" Dani yelled.

Maya ended the call. She put on a brave face and walked back to the door. She cracked the chain lock. "Sorry about that. Listen, I am interested in information about a .357 Desert Eagle Automatic. The serial number is filed off and has a cracked handle."

"It sounds like a gun I sold last week," the man said in a slight Russian accent. "How about I come in and we can talk about it."

Maya got a chance to look at the stranger at the door. He was tall, about six-feet, dreamy blue eyes, Caucasian, medium build, and dark hair with a receding hairline. He appeared to be in his early forties. For an older man, he was handsome.

"No. That's okay, we can talk here," Maya said. "What can you tell me about who sold the gun?"

"People like that don't like to give out names."

"Well, what did he or she look like?"

"I wasn't paying much attention," the man said. "Why don't you let me come in and we can talk about it?"

"Look, that was the reason I gave out the flyer, to collect information. So far, you have not told me anything. What color is the handle?"

"Why don't you open the door and we can go out, have a drink, and grab some lunch? I can tell you the color and even what's on it."

Maya pepped up. It was obvious he knew something. But he had the kind of mean, dead look that you would not want to meet in a dark alley. "Tell me here or leave." She tried to close the door.

The man stuck a foot in the door to block it. "Oh, come on," he said with a mischievous grin. "Don't be like that. You want to find the owner of the gun, don't you? I want to help."

Maya pushed back on the door, but the stranger was stronger. "If you don't take your foot of the door, I'm calling the police."

A moment later, the stranger forcefully pushed the door open. Maya found herself face-to-face with the stranger. Her heart beat was racing a mile-a-minute. He clasped his gloved hands together. She swallowed the lump in her throat. She could see her life flash before her eyes. He closed the small space between them. Her small, petite frame looked up at him. She noticed a small scar underneath his chin. A large tattoo of a skull and cross bone covered the back of his left hand, just like on the gun. He was the owner.

"Tell me about the .357 Desert Eagle," the man said.

Maya was shaking like a leaf on a tree. She was scared but she managed to find her voice. "Why don't you tell me? I think you know more about it than I do."

"I'm not going to play games with you," the man said.

Without warning, Maya felt a large, strong hand around her neck. She struggled but it was no use. "Let go of me!" She began clawing at his hands.

The man began dragging her toward the door. "Why don't we take a little ride?"

"I said let go!" Maya tried stomping down on his foot, but the mountain did not move.

"The woman said let her go," the voice said from the doorway.

Maya looked around to see Victor standing in the doorway. She'd never been so happy to see anyone in her life. She took the chance to get out of the vise grip.

The stranger raised his hand in a surrendering motion. A sly grin crossed his face. "I don't want no trouble."

Victor marched over and got in the man's face. "You got trouble. What do you want?"

Maya rubbed her neck. "He wanted to know about the .357."

"What do you know about the .357?" Victor asked.

The man began backing up toward the door. "I don't know anything. I thought I may have sold that gun to the killer, that's all."

"How did you know to come here?" Victor asked. "Who did you sell it to?"

"He's the owner," Maya yelled from across the room.

"Did you kill Montgomery Sterling?" Victor asked.

Instead of answering the man made a mad dash out the door. Victor was hot on his trail. He managed to tackle him on the front lawn. The two men began to wrestle around. The stranger managed to get on top of Victor but not for long. He flipped the man off him.

The man landed on his feet and tried to run away again. Victor tackled him once more, but this time, he managed to land a punch to the man's jaw. "Who are you? Who hired you?"

"Take your dirty hands off me, right now," the man said through clenched teeth.

Victor didn't miss the Russian accent. He grabbed the man by the collar to his feet. The stranger took the opportunity to land a martial art blow to Victor's chest. He fell to the ground with a thud.

Victor looked to see the man running down the street. His long black coat flapping in the wind. He got the best of him this time around, but he was sure they would meet again.

"Victor, are you alright?" Maya said, rushing to his side.

Victor began brushing the grass from his clothes. "Yeah, I'm fine. What about you? Are you alright? Did he hurt you?"

"My neck is a little sore," Maya said. "But I'll live."

"Good. We need to give a sketch to the police," Victor said. "I have a feeling your visitor is not a good Samaritan."

"He was scary," Maya said. "I know what you mean now about weirdos. It's a good thing that you showed up when you did."

"Come on." Victor escorted her toward his truck. "We need to report this to the police. It's best to do it while it's still fresh in your mind."

You don't have to worry," Maya said. "I can never forget that face. But we can't go right now."

"Why not?"

"Someone named Abbey Knowles also called me about the gun," Maya said. "I'm supposed to meet her at the Old Fisherman's Wharf."

Victor leaned back. "When?"

"In about an hour."

"Let's go," Victor said, leading Maya toward the truck.

***

Priest watched from the end of the block as Victor and Maya got into the truck. He could have taken care of her if he was not interrupted. He was the same man that showed up at the Boys Club. Whoever he was, he gave the appearance that he was not to be taken lightly. He was sure that Abbey reached out to her. His job just got a little harder. That was fine with him; he liked a challenge.

He watched as the truck pulled from the driveway and headed toward him. He slid down in the seat. As the vehicle vanished from view, he pushed the ignition button and followed close behind.

***

"She said five o'clock," Maya said, walking to and fro in front of the abandoned building. "She's late."

"Are you sure this is the place?" Victor asked.

"I'm positive," Maya answered. "Traffic is terrible this time of day."

"I just hope she is able to shed some light on who she sold that gun to," Victor said.

"I think it was the Russian that showed up at the house," Maya said. "Who the hell is he?"

"I don't know but I'm going to find out. I'm sure it was him," Victor said. "Abbey may be able to confirm if she sold the gun to him. I'm glad you are okay. You never should have opened the door."

"I didn't," Maya argued. "I told you, he pushed it open. Where's Paul?" she asked, changing the subject.

"He's watching videos of the night Dani was at Cadence," Victor explained. "Hopefully, someone will remember seeing her in another club or bar the night of the murder."

"Anything on the video?" Maya asked.

"Nothing so far," Victor said. "I have a feeling it will just tell us she left the club before nine o'clock."

100

A moment later a beat-up red Volkswagen pulled alongside the empty building. The blonde-haired woman opened the door and got out.

"Maya, this must be your caller," Victor said.

"Maya?" the woman called.

"Abbey?" Maya called back. "We thought you weren't coming."

Victor noticed the woman looked nervous. He understood. Coming forward was a difficult thing to do. He strolled toward Abbey. She flashed him a weak smile.

As he walked closer, he spotted a brown Impala behind Abbey speeding toward her.

"Look out!" Victor yelled. He moved in and whisked Abbey to safety. He rolled over to see the vehicle driving recklessly away.

"Who the hell was that?" Abbey asked, stumbling to her feet.

"It's the Russian that showed up at my house," Maya said, running over to help. "I got a good look at him. That's him." She kneeled next to Abbey. "Are you alright?"

"No. I'm not alright," Abbey said, tossing her long blonde hair over her right shoulder.

"He must have followed us here," Maya said.

"You think?" Abbey cried. "I could have been killed."

"But you weren't," Victor threw in. "We need to talk to you."

"Yeah, well, I just decided that I'm not talking," Abbey cried. "I didn't sign up for this."

"My sister needs your testimony about the gun," Maya argued.

"I need to live," Abbey threw back.

"You think you're safe?" Victor said. "He knows who you are. Your life is already in danger. Why don't you tell us what you know? We can get you protection?"

"No thank you." Abbey turned to leave.

"What the hell is wrong with you?" Victor exclaimed. Abbey turned back around.

"Do you think this is a game?" Victor strolled toward Abbey. "I guarantee you that this is not. That man is a hired killer. A professional. He will not stop until he gets what he wants. You do not need to be running around alone."

"I'm not running around," Abbey said.

"What are you going to do?" Maya asked.

"I'm on my way out of town," Abbey said. "I thought I was going to collect some extra money for the trip, but it's not worth my life. I'm out of here."

"So, you're just going to run away?" Victor asked.

"That's exactly what I'm going to do," Abbey said. "Good luck!" She hurried toward her vehicle, opened the door, got in, and drove away.

The duo stood in silence.

Maya was the first to speak." Can she do that?"

"Yes, she can," Victor answered.

"She was our best possible lead," Maya argued. "We shouldn't have let her go."

"What are we going to do?" Victor asked. "Tie her down. Let's go."

***

The next morning, Spencer let himself into his father's house. He made his way into the living room. He discovered his stepmother standing in the middle of the room. She was beautiful as ever. He suddenly took her in his arms. He pressed his lips to hers. He'd been going crazy the past couple of days not being able to see her.

"I have missed you," Spencer said on a long sigh. He was doing his best to control himself. He knew it was wrong. He didn't care. He was in love with his father's wife. "I wanted to see you, but I couldn't take the chance."

"You were worried about me?" Paula asked.

"You know I was," Spencer replied.

"You think I did it?" Paula asked.

"I wouldn't blame you if you did," Spencer said.

"You really think I killed him?"

"Didn't you?"

"No," Paula answered. "I thought you killed him."

Spencer leaned back in surprise.

Paula searched his face. A faint smile crossed her lovely face. "Look at you. You lie so well. I have to rethink all the things you have told me!"

Spencer recaptured her lips.

The sound of someone clearing their throat from across the room caused the couple to pull apart.

"I hope that I didn't interrupt anything," Tonya said, strolling further into the room. "You two look so cozy."

"Who are you?" Spencer asked, wiping the lipstick from his lips.

"This is Tonya Sims," Paula answered for Spencer. "She's Dani McCall's attorney."

"What do you want?" Spencer asked.

"Actually, I'm following up on some questions from the other day."

"Is there anything new on the case?" Paula asked.

"Nothing yet. I have more questions," Tonya said.

"We don't have to talk to you," Spencer replied. "You're not the police."

"You can talk to me now," Tonya walked further into the room, "or you can wait until I get you on the stand and you can answer questions about you and your stepmother."

Spencer looked like he wanted to slink away. "I don't have to explain myself to you or anyone else."

"Not now," Tonya quipped.

"I'm done talking to you," Spencer said.

"Sounds like you're still pissed after talking to my brother," Tonya answered.

"Your brother?" Spencer asked.

"Victor Sexton," Tonya answered. "He's my private investigator. I heard you had quite an interesting conversation with him."

"I had nothing to say to him," Sterling said. "And nothing to say to you. I'll be in the office." He stormed out of the room.

Paula took a seat on the arm of the antique chair. She crossed one leg over the other. "Okay, ask away. I just hope you ask better questions than you did the other day."

"I hope so," Tonya said. "Let's begin with the phone call that you made on the night of the murder."

"What phone call?"

"The one you made to your stepson."

"My stepson?"

"Yes. The phone records show that you placed a call to your stepson around the time that your husband was killed. It was made just two minutes before the call to the police."

"Where is this going?"

"You will know when you tell me why you placed the call."

Paula stood. "I was in the bathtub. I didn't call anyone. My husband used my phone to tell him that he changed his mind about going to New York."

"That's funny because the answering service operator remembers taking a call from you. She said that you stated it was an emergency. What was the emergency?"

"Well, she is mistaken," Paula said. "I said no such thing. It's not the first time a service took down the wrong message. Now if there is nothing else, we are done here."

"For the moment," Tonya said. She was about to leave the room when she noticed the beautiful, expensive diamond bracelet on her wrist. "Beautiful bracelet. Where did you get it?"

"Levine's," Paula answered. "My husband gave it to me on our fifth anniversary."

"He had good taste," Tonya said. She headed back down the hallway. She looked in the office on the right to find Spencer sitting at his father's desk. He seemed to be going through some files. She strolled inside. "You look comfortable in your father's chair."

Spencer tilted his head to one side. He was clearly annoyed. "I am very comfortable, Mrs. Sims. What can I do for you?"

"Okay. I will get straight to the point," Tonya said. "I was wondering why your stepmother called you on the night of the murder."

Spencer let out a low sigh. "Didn't you ask her that question?"

"I did," Tonya said. "Now I am asking you."

"Why? To see if we have the same answer."

"Exactly."

"Why do you want to know what we talked about?"

"Because I want to know who hired the killer that killed your father," Tonya said. Without another word, she turned and headed toward the door. She suddenly refocused on Spencer. "Oh, one more thing. It would be better for you and your stepmother to get your stories straight before the trial."

Tonya walked back to her car and slid behind the wheel. She removed the cell phone from her large, black bag. She quickly punched in Dominique's number. Her future sister-in-law answered on the fourth ring. "Dominique? What are you doing?"

Chapter Eight

Several hours later, Tonya opened the door to Levine's Jewelers.

Dominique brought up the rear. "You caught them together?"

"They were kissing," Tonya said. "I knew that she didn't love her husband but to fool around with his son… That is a new low," she whispered.

"I wonder how long it has been going on," Dominique whispered back. "Poor man. I wonder if he knew."

"I bet he didn't," Tonya said. "If he did, he would have bounced both of them out without a dime."

"You think they may have hired the killer?" Dominique asked.

"That's exactly what I think," Tonya said. She headed toward the glass counter.

"I don't think we should be doing this," Dominque said. "We should leave this to Victor or Paul."

"This is exactly what we should be doing." Tonya said. "Don't worry. I just need to check something out. This store sells unique pieces of jewelry to high class customers. That bracelet Mrs. Sterling is wearing is quite unique. I'm sure I saw it here."

The saleswoman walked over to them. "Good afternoon, ladies. Are you looking for something in particular?"

"Right now, we are just looking," Tonya answered.

"Take your time," the woman said. She strolled to the end of the counter to help an older gentleman.

"What are we looking for?" Dominique asked.

"I'll know it when I see it," Tonya said. She looked over the beautiful pieces of jewelry until she spotted the exact piece Mrs. Montgomery was wearing. "Found it."

Dominque hurried over.

"Juste Un Clou White Gold," Tonya read.

Dominique gasped. She leaned over and whispered, "White Gold Bracelet? Talk about expensive."

"The one Mrs. Sterling was wearing had to be around three-hundred-and-forty-thousand dollars."

"She could have bought it herself," Dominique said.

Tonya chuckled. "I doubt it. Mrs. Sterling is not the type to treat herself." She shook her head. "No. Someone bought her that bracelet. I just need to find out who." She waved the saleswoman over. "Can we see this piece?"

"I only had a couple in the store," the clerk said. "I sold both. I can order one for you, if you want."

"No. Actually, I need some information."

The young lady looked nervous. "What kind of information?"

"We don't want to scare you but it's a matter of life and death," Dominique said.

"What?" the clerk inquired.

"Don't be scared," Tonya said.

"Look, I don't know what is going on here," the young lady began. "I am not allowed to give out any information on our customers. I could lose my job."

Tonya leaned over and patted the lady's hand in comfort. "I'm an attorney. You and the store are not in any trouble. You will not lose your job. I'm going to ask you a question."

The clerk's eyes stretched.

"Do you know Montgomery Sterling?" Tonya asked.

"The man that was killed?" the clerk asked. "Yes. I know him. He's one of our customers."

"By any chance did you sell a Juste Un Clou White Gold bracelet to Montgomery Sterling?"

She appeared to be in thought for a moment before she responded, "No."

Tonya glanced at Dominque. "No!"

"What did the buyer look like?" Dominique asked.

"I never forget a good-looking man," she said. "You said it is a matter of life and death?"

"It is," Tonya answered.

"We wouldn't ask if it wasn't," Dominique said.

"Alright. I will tell you," she said. "The person that bought the bracelet was Spencer Sterling. He was the one that bought it, not his father."

***

Tonya let herself into the house. The living room was dark. She fumbled for the lamp switch on the end table. Stephen was already in bed. She removed her shoes and quietly headed up the stairs. A moment later, the light came on, and Stephen appeared at the top of the stairs.

"Where have you been?" Stephen asked. "I've been worried about you."

Tonya swallowed the lump in her throat. "I have been working on the case."

"Doing what? It's almost ten o'clock."

Tonya leaned back in surprise. Stephen never raised his voice. "Investigative work."

"Investigative work?" Stephen repeated. "I thought that is what your brother is supposed to be doing."

"He is." Tonya started up the stairs. "I just followed up on a lead, that's all."

"You told me that you wouldn't be doing anything dangerous."

"I'm not," Tonya defended "It's pertaining to the case, so I had to follow up on it."

"I don't like it," Stephen said, turning and heading back into the master bedroom.

"Like what, Stephen?"

He swirled back to Tonya. She sensed that he was trying his best to control his anger. He ran a large hand over his low haircut.

She tossed the shoes and purse in the chair. "I know what this is about. You still don't like the idea of me taking this case. Being, uh, uh a defense attorney again."

"I didn't say that."

"You didn't have to," Tonya said. "I can read between the lines. You have been acting distance since I took Dani's case."

"That's not true," Stephen said.

"Yes, it is," Tonya argued. "You have been working late the past couple of days."

"I'm working on a Manson project," Stephen said. "I landed that before you took this case. What about the kids?"

"What about them?" Tonya asked. "I explained to them what Mommy was doing."

Stephen smirked. He shook his head. "This is what I was afraid of. I knew when you took this case that you would forget about me and the kids."

"That's not true," Tonya threw back. "Why are you doing this?"

"I should ask you that question," Stephen said. "When we got married you promised that you would give up being a defense attorney, that you would be my wife and a mother to our children." He pointed at Tonya. "That's what you promised."

"I have kept that promise, Stephen," Tonya threw back. "But a friend, a sorority sister, needed my help, and I'm going to help her. You should know something about that. Didn't you help your frat brother William when he needed help?"

"It's not the same thing," Stephen said.

"Why isn't it?" Tonya asked. "If you ask me it's more important. I'm trying to keep someone out of jail. You helped someone get a job."

"Now you think your work is more important," Stephen said.

Tonya turned her back. "I never said that. What is the big deal? It's one case."

"Your brother is opening a private investigation agency."

Tonya turned back around. "What does that have to do with me?"

"Come on, Tonya," Stephen said. "He may try to talk you into defending other clients."

"He won't," Tonya said. "He was worried about me taking this case."

"Good. Don't even think about it," Stephen threatened. "The kids are too young. They need their mother." He tossed back the comforter. "I guess that I can understand you wanting to help your friend." He slipped down between the sheets. "What's her name?"

"Dani McCall," Tonya answered. "She's the anchorwoman for channel 4."

"I never watch that channel," Stephen said. "How long is the case?"

"I don't know," Tonya said. "We are still investigating."

Stephen fluffed his pillow. He yawned. "Don't take too long."

Tonya didn't need to hear another word. She gathered her shoes and purse. She stormed out of the bedroom, walked down the hall, and into the guest bedroom. "Jerk."

***

"Stay out of this case," Victor said to Dominique. He walked inside his office. He noticed a few pieces of office furniture. "What?"

"I picked them out," Dominique said, sitting in one of the oval black chairs. "What do you think?"

"They're nice. Don't change the subject."

"I'm not changing the subject," Dominique said. "They should work for now. Also, the phones should be working tomorrow. The printers and computers will be here around two. I'm working with a very renowned interior decorator. This place has lots of potential."

"Just remember, I don't have a lot of money," Victor said nonchalantly.

"I have a little saved up," Dominique said.

"I don't want your money."

"I will give it anyway," Dominique said. "So, let me."

Victor looked at her for a moment. It was difficult to say 'no' to her. He chuckled.

"What's so funny?"

"You and Tonya together."

Dominique placed her hands on her hips. "I helped you solve your last case with the military."

"I remember it differently."

Dominque walked over to an empty space in the outer office. "I think we should put a large plant here and one over there. VSI in big bold letters here. Photos on this wall and the opposite wall. Renaissance. Andy Warhol? I will talk it over with the decorator."

"Whatever you say." He walked into what he thought was an empty office. He couldn't help but notice Dominique had been busy. There was a desk with a lamp, chair, table and a large white board. "I see you already struck in here."

"It's not much. But it will work for now."

Victor took a seat in the chair behind the desk. He opened the file of the case to go over the notes and police reports once again.

"Tonya and I solved the case. We know who hired the killer," Dominique said.

Victor's head snapped up. "You and Tonya know who hired the killer?"

"That's right."

Victor leaned back in the chair. "Who hired the killer?"

"From what we deduced at the jewelers," Dominique began.

"Deduced?"

"Yes, deduced." Dominique grinned. "We believe it was Spencer Sterling."

"What makes you think the son did it?"

"Easy." Dominique began. "He bought an expensive bracelet that his stepmother wears proudly. I mean, I can't blame him. It's a beautiful piece of jewelry. Expensive. Exquisite. If someone bought me something like that, I'd wear it, too."

"Someone?"

Dominique slapped Victor on the arm. "You know what I mean."

"That doesn't mean that he had his father killed."

"He's having an affair with his stepmother," Dominique said. "Tonya caught them together today. Red handed. They were kissing."

"If that is true, it gives them a motive. But you need evidence to prove that they had him knocked off."

"What about the bracelet?"

"He could have bought it as a gift," Victor said. "Which he probably did, but it's still kind of flimsy. We need something more concrete. We haven't found it yet." He closed the folder in frustration. "We need to find a way to connect them to the killer."

He strolled over to the window and looked at the Washington Monument standing out against the city skyline. The son and stepmother looked guilty. He wasn't surprised about the affair. Spencer was the kind of man that would covet his father's wife because of the way he treated him. He was a tool. But he didn't come across as a killer. Why would they chance it? If they were caught, they would lose everything.

Victor's mind went to Abbey. He was worried about her. He had to find her. She was frightened. She had reason to be. The information she had could be crucial. He had to find out what she knew. A friend from the Department of Motor Vehicles was able to give him Abbey's home address. Paul was watching the house for any sight of her; so far, she hasn't shown up.

Victor picked up the mobile phone and punched in Paul's number. He answered on the third ring.

"Colonel?"

"Anything yet?"

"No. Still no sign of Abbey," Paul said. "I confirmed with the neighbors to see if she still lives at this address. She does. She lives with her grandmother. I spoke with her earlier. She hasn't seen her granddaughter since last night. I fear the worst."

"Let's hope for the best," Victor said. "Stay on it for a couple more hours. I'll replace you."

"I'm getting hungry," Paul confessed.

"I know. I'm afraid it will just be you and me for a while," Victor said. "Until I hire more investigators."

"It's okay, Colonel," Paul said. "I'm just grateful for the work."

"I'll see you later." Victor ended the call. He looked to see Dominique's bewildered expression.

"I was talking," Dominique chastised. "What did Paul say?"

"No one has seen or heard from Abbey since the accident," Victor explained.

"The information that she has about the weapon can help the case," Dominique said.

"I should have been firmer," Victor said. "I never should have let her go."

"You tried to stop her," Dominque said. "She wanted to leave. You cannot make her take protection if she doesn't want it. Besides, you are making up for it by trying to find her."

Victor's phone rang again. He recognized Detective West's number. "West. What do you have for me?" He listened a moment. "Interesting. I have someone watching her house." He stood. "I'm on my way out the door." He clicked off the call. "Gotta go, baby." He strolled over and planted a quick kiss on Dominique's lips. "Sweet."

"What's going on now?" Dominique whined.

"I'm meeting Detective West at the station," Victor answered. "Then I'm replacing Paul on stakeout." He headed toward the door.

"Victor?" Dominique called after him.

"I will see you in the morning." With a wave, Victor was out the door.

"What have I done?" Dominique said aloud.

***

"The man that you fought with and almost ran you down is Konovalov Petrovich, also known as Priest," Detective West explained, handing Victor the photo.

Victor's eyes scanned the picture of the familiar face. "That's him."

"He's a hired killer," Detective West said. "He was once a part of the Zakharovich Crime Family."

"He worked for Sabantsev Makar? What happened?" Victor asked. "Once you're in, you don't just walk out."

114

"No one knows for sure," Detective West said. "He still does some work for them from time-to-time."

"Then why isn't he behind bars?"

"You know as well as I do that it's hard to find anyone that wants to testify against these guys," Detective West said. "No one sees or hears anything. Look at what happened with Abbey Knowles. He scared her to death. It happens."

"I know," Victor said. "But I will get him."

"Wait a moment," Detective West said. "No one wants to see him behind bars more than I do. You just remember we would like for him to testify."

"You mean you want him to tell us what he knows about the Zakharovich family?" Victor said. "C'mon. You know that is a long shot. Men like Priest will never turn snitch. He'll take what he knows to the grave."

"It could happen," Detective West said. He placed the photo on the desk. "What about Abbey Knowles? Any word on where she might be?"

No." Victor glanced at his watch. "I better get going. I'm replacing Paul on stakeout. He's starving."

"Alright, if I hear anything else, I will give you a call," Detective West said, walking Victor out in the main area.

"Thanks," Victor said.

***

Thirty minutes later, Victor pecked on the passenger side window of Paul's car. He leaned over and opened the door. He slid in the passenger's seat. "Any sign of Abbey?"

"No. Not yet," Paul said. "I'm beginning to think she's not coming back. I have been here for hours and there is no sign of her. I bet she is long gone by now."

Victor glanced at the house. The only light was from a television. "She lives with the grandmother?"

"Yes."

115

"What about the back of the house?" Victor asked. "Did you check it out?"

Paul frowned. "I can see everything from here."

"How do we know that Abbey didn't sneak in the back way?" Victor asked. "I'm looking at a pair of stairs along the side of the house."

"I can guarantee that she didn't use them while I have been out here."

Victor's phone rang. He recognized his brother's number. "Yeah, Gerald. Really? The Red Door? The bartender, Luis Orchard remembers Dani. Has he spoken to Tonya?" He glanced over to see Paul throwing up his hands in happiness. "Sounds good. We'll talk to him later. Keep me posted." He ended the call.

"Sounds like good news," Paul said. He examined Victor's face. "Shouldn't you be jumping up and down? Dani McCall may have an alibi."

"It's good news but let's not put the cart before the horse," Victor said. "Let's wait and see what the bartender has to say. See if his story checks out. Besides, it really doesn't matter at this point. Even if he gives her an alibi, she could have hired him. We must find out who did the hiring."

"Gerald managed to do something I couldn't even do," Paul said. "I got nowhere with the club owners. They treated me like I had the plague, especially Luis Orchard."

Victor chuckled. "Don't take it personal. They know Gerald, that's all."

"Well, as long as we got the information we needed, I will try not to take it personal."

"On another subject," Victor said. "I spoke with Detective West today."

"About the case?" Paul asked.

"Yes. I got a chance to look at the victim's body. There is no doubt it was a professional hit. It looks like it was a

Russian hitman by the name of Konovalov Petrovich. He also goes by the name of Priest. He was once a part of the Zakharovich Crime Family."

Paul whistled. "The Zakharovich Crime Family? That's huge. Who would be stupid enough to be involved with those guys?"

"Exactly," Victor said. He quickly filled Paul in on what Detective West told him.

"It could have been any of the suspects," Paul said.

"All we have to do is follow the money," Victor said. "It will lead us to who hired Priest."

"I cannot argue with you on that," Paul said.

"Detective West wants VSI to work with the police department on some cases," Victor said out of the blue.

Paul glanced alongside Victor's head. "VSI?"

"That's the name of my agency."

"Then this is real," Paul said. "You're really going to open your own agency?"

"What do you think we have been doing here?" Victor asked.

"Tonya only spoke about this case and Dominique couldn't really tell me much."

"Well, I'm telling you," Victor said. "VSI is moving forward. I would like for you to be a part of it. What will Kayla think about you doing this kind of work?"

"Kayla will just be glad that I have a full-time job," Paul said. "It is full-time, isn't it? With benefits?"

Victor chuckled. "As long as we have work, it's full-time. In our line of work, we need benefits."

"I have something to look forward to besides my pension," Paul said. "I'm not as fast as I use to be since I was shot in the chest, but I'm working on it. The rehabilitation has been good. Productive."

"Paul, as long as you can pass the background check and you're able to carry a concealed weapon, then it's fine."

"Like you, I was a sniper," Paul said.

"You also know logistics and how to make a bomb," Victor said.

Paul leaned back. "How did you know that?"

"General Goss came to see me a while back," Victor said, looking out the windshield. "He was recruiting for a secret government agency that he runs. He wanted to take you on."

"You're kidding," Paul said. "He didn't say anything to me."

"I told him not to," Victor answered.

"Why?"

"You weren't ready yet," Victor said. "You were just beginning rehab."

"I was a mess back then," Paul said. "Luckily, I have Kayla. You and the rest of the family have been very supportive. Why didn't you accept the General's offer?"

"I wasn't interested," Victor answered. "I have a feeling that we will be hearing from General Goss, especially with the talent that I plan to assemble with VSI."

Paul grinned. "Something tells me I am in for a wild ride."

"Buckle up," Victor said. "It's going to be an adventure."

What about Tonya?" Paul asked. "I thought she gave up criminal law to raise a family?"

"She did," Victor answered. "I think she's having second thoughts."

"How does Stephen feel about this whole thing?"

"He's not very happy about it."

Paul shook his head. "I hope they work it out."

"Me, too," Victor said. "Why don't you head on home? Grab something to eat. I'll take over."

"I'm starving," Paul said. "All I had for lunch was a tuna sandwich, a bag of chips, and a soda."

"Get going," Victor said, opening the door to exit the vehicle.

"Colonel. Look!" Paul exclaimed.

Victor looked to see a small hooded figure, covered in darkness, moving toward the side of the house.

"Looks like you were right," Paul said.

"I told you, she wasn't leaving town," Victor said. "Let's go."

"Two black men sneaking around a neighbor's house this time of night," Paul joked. "Are you sure you want to do this?"

"No. But we have no other choice." Victor jogged across the street.

"I knew you were going to say that," Paul said, following him.

Abbey spotted them heading toward her. She made a beeline in the opposite direction. Paul was too fast for her. He grabbed her by the arm. She tried to struggle.

"Tell your handler to let go of me or I swear I will scream," Abbey threatened.

"Go ahead. Scream."

"Fine." Abbey opened her mouth to scream.

Victor quickly cover her mouth with a large hand. "I wouldn't do that if I were you."

Abbey's mouth was moving, but not a sound was coming out.

"What?" Victor taunted. "I can't hear you. Stop talking. Don't scream. I will uncover your mouth. Got it?"

Abbey nodded.

"Good," Victor said.

"I told you before that I'm not talking to you about anything," Abbey said.

"Why did you agree to meet with Maya?" Paul asked.

"I told you, I thought I could use the extra money," Abbey said. "But I'm not willing to die for it."

"You're coming with us," Victor said. He attempted to guide her in the opposite direction "He knows who you are. By now he knows where you live. You're not safe here."

"We'll protect you and your grandmother," Paul said.

Abbey loosened Victor's vice grip. "I told you to forget it. Me and my grandmother will be just fine." She rushed up the steps. "Forget about us."

Victor started up after her.

"Boss. Let her go," Paul said after Victor.

Victor stopped in mid-stride. "She needs protection."

"She doesn't want it."

"That doesn't mean that we give up." Victor looked to see Abbey closing the door. She gave him a quick wave, closed the door, and vanished.

"See. This is a waste of time," Paul said.

"I'll watch from across the street," Victor said. "Head home."

"Okay, I'm out of here."

Chapter Nine

Priest watched from the wooded area on the side of Abbey's house. He wasn't surprised to see Victor Sexton there. He found out who he was, a former Special Ops and former Commander of CID. It didn't matter. The mission was the same. Abbey Knowles was a liability; she had to be disposed of.

He watched as Abbey continued up the step and into her house as Victor and another man walked away. A moment later, a light appeared in the bedroom. The curtains were drawn but he could see the silhouette of her moving back and forth.

Priest took a drag of his cigarette. He tossed the butt to the ground. He stepped on it and covered it with dirt. He placed the silencer on the .357 Desert Eagle Automatic and waited patiently for the target to reappear. A few minutes later, Abbey moved in front of the window and Priest pulled the trigger. The shadowy figure dropped. With a look of satisfaction on his face, Priest walked away. The job was done.

***

The sound of breaking glass caused Victor and Paul to run back toward the house. He pointed to his cousin to take the front. His long legs hurried up the steps two at a time. He opened the window and hurried inside. Adrenaline was pumping through him. It has been a long time since he said a prayer; now was as good as time as any. He was prepared to find Abbey, but when he turned the body over, it was a young man. He was lying face down in the middle of the floor in a pool of blood. He glanced over to find her cowered in a corner. She appeared to be in a daze.

The bedroom door flew open. He came face to face with a bewildered looking Paul. He stopped dead in his tracks. "Oh no." His eyes panned over to Abbey. He breathed a sigh of relief. "Abbey?"

"She's in a daze," Victor answered.

Victor placed a finger underneath the victim's nose for any signs of life. He wasn't expecting to find it. He knew he was dead. "He's gone."

"Abbey, baby," the grandmother's tiny voice called from the hallway. "What's all that noise?"

"I'm going after him." Paul turned to leave.

"Don't bother," Victor said. "He's long gone by now. He's a professional, remember? Make sure the grandmother doesn't come in," Victor ordered. "I don't want her to see this."

"I'll lead her back downstairs and call 911," Paul said.

"Thank you." Victor needed answers. He moved over to Abbey. The color had drained from her face. Her skin was white as a ghost. She was shaking. "Abbey? Who was he?"

Abbey didn't answer. She looked straight ahead. It was as if he wasn't there.

Victor shook her. "Abbey, snap out of it."

Abbey slowly looked into Victor's face. She finally spoke. "His name is Ricky Hunter. He was my boyfriend." She broke down and began to weep.

Victor could feel the pain bouncing threw her body. "I'm so sorry, Abbey."

"It's my fault!" Abbey wailed. "It's all my fault!"

The sound of sirens could be heard blaring in the background. "The police are here," Victor announced. "We need to go."

"No!" Abbey yelled. On hands and knees, she crawled over to her boyfriend's lifeless body. "I want to stay with Ricky."

Victor pulled her to her feet. "There is nothing that you can do for him now." He dragged her from the bedroom, down the stairs, and out the front door.

"What happened?" Detective West asked, exiting the police cruiser.

"There is a body upstairs?" Victor explained. "It was Priest."

***

"He stood here and watched," Victor said to Detective West. He pointed the flashlight over a fresh set of footprints. He glanced around carefully. He pushed aside a small stack of leaves with his foot. He uncovered a cigarette butt. "Hand me an evidence bag." Bending down, he picked it up with a pair of tweezers and smelled it. "It's still fresh." He placed it in the bag. "This is just a formality. We know who did it."

"This is where he shot from?" Detective West asked. He looked at the distance from the woods to the house. "What is that? Twenty-five yards? That is further than old man Sterling."

"Exactly. One shot," Victor echoed.

"Men like Priest are worth the money," Detective West said.

"There is only one thing wrong this time," Victor said.

"He shot the wrong person," Detective West pointed out.

"Sort of," Victor said.

"Sort of?" Detective West repeated.

123

"I know that. You know that, but Priest doesn't know that."

"What are you thinking?"

"I think we can use this to our advantage," Victor said.

Detective West rubbed a hand underneath his chin. "You mean release the name of the victim as Abbey Knowles instead of the actual victim."

"Exactly," Victor said. "So far no one besides us has seen the victim."

"I don't know," Detective West said. "I would have to run it by the Captain."

"I'm sure he will go along with it," Victor said. "You and I both know that if Priest finds out that Abbey is still alive, he will come after her. I'm not willing to take that chance. Are you?"

Detective West thought a moment. "Look, I'm all in but like I said, let's see what the Captain says."

"That's all I ask," Victor said.

"What about the grandmother?" Detective West asked.

"That's where you come in," Victor said. "She doesn't see or hear too well. I figured you can try to explain it to her. Maybe tell her that Abbey went out of town." He shrugged. "Which, she was going to do anyway."

"What about police protection for Ms. Knowles?" Detective West asked.

"I know a place where she can stay until this is over," Victor said.

"Care to tell me where that is?" Detective West asked. "I need to question her about what happened while everything is fresh in her mind."

"How about in the morning?" Victor answered. "I'll give you the address. You can talk to her there."

"Or you can bring her by the station," Detective West said with a fake smile.

"She has been through too much," Victor argued. "I don't want to do that to her."

"That wasn't a request," Detective West said.

"It is if you want to speak to her," Victor threw back. He looked around the wooded area. "It's too dark. We can't really see anything. It will be better in the morning."

They walked to the back of the house to see Paul headed toward them.

"Ten o'clock," Detective West pointed at Victor. "I will call you on that other issue that we discussed." He strolled over to join the other officers.

"We will be there, Detective," Victor said after him.

Detective West threw up a hand in acknowledgement. Victor focused on Paul. "How is she?"

"She hasn't said a word since I put her in the car," Paul answered. "She just sits and stares out the window."

"That's understandable." Victor took a deep breath. "I'll take her to the safe house. I'll see you in the morning."

"See you then, boss," Paul said, heading to his vehicle.

***

"What are you doing here?" Victor asked Dominique. She was making up a spare bedroom at the Gaithersburg house.

"That's a stupid question." Dominique fluffed the pillow and turned down the comforter. "You phoned and told me that you were bringing Abbey here. You needed help. I am here to help. I wasn't that far away. I figured that I would come over and see what I could do. Dani and Maya have gone to bed." Her eyes landed on the young lady next to Victor, holding tight to a black backpack.

"Dominique, this is Abbey Knowles," Victor said. "Abbey this is my fiancé, Dominique Frazier. She's also a nurse."

A smile crossed Dominique's face. "Hello, Abbey. It's a pleasure to meet you. I'm sorry for your loss." She took the

125

young woman by the hand. "Come on in. I made up this room for you. It's not much. Victor doesn't like to decorate, but feel free to make it your room for as long as you need it."

"Did you catch him?" Abbey snapped at Victor.

Victor's heart dropped in his chest. He believed in being honest, no matter how much it hurt. "No. Priest got away."

"No one knows where this Priest is?" Abbey asked.

"We have half of the police department out looking for him," Victor said. "It's a matter of time. We'll find him."

"I hope so," Abbey said.

"It would go faster, Abbey, if you tell me what you know."

"Victor do you have to do that now?" Dominique asked. "She has really gone through a lot tonight. Can't it wait until morning?"

"I really don't know anything," Abbey said in a soft voice. "This man came into the pawnshop where I work. He bought a .357 Desert Eagle Automatic. I didn't really pay attention to him. I just remember the gun. We don't get many of them. The gun had a white chrome handle and a skull and cross bones on it. When I read the flyer saying it may have been used to kill that news station owner, Mr. Sterling, and there was a reward, I thought why not get something out of it. I talked it over with Ricky." She dropped her head. "He said we can get the money and head out to California like we always talked about." She sat on the foot of the bed. "Poor Ricky. No one deserves to die like that." She wiped her eyes with the back of her hand.

"Did you create a record of the sale for the gun?" Victor inquired.

Abbey gave Victor an 'are you kidding' look.

"Most pawnshops that sell questionable items don't keep records of the sales," Victor said.

"Before Devin hired me. You're right. He didn't keep good records at all. His bookkeeping was awful. Just awful. I turned things around," Abbey said.

Victor pepped up. "You mean you may have a receipt for the sale of this particular gun?"

"I told Devin if he wanted me to work for him, I would keep better records."

"He agreed to that?" Dominique asked.

"Devin didn't care. The records are not one hundred percent," Abbey said, "but pretty damn close. I know for sure that I have a record for the gun that killed Mr. Sterling."

"That's what you were going to give to Maya?" Victor asked.

"Yes."

"How did you get that information?" Victor asked. "Men like Priest don't give that kind of information out."

"I know," Abbey said. "The day he came in the shop, when he went in the back to talk to Devin, I went out front and got his license plate number. He got into a 2017 silver Ford SUV. I have a friend that runs plates. It was a rental. Hertz. I smooth talked them into giving me the name and address of the person that rented the car. From that information, I created a sales slip."

Victor looked at Dominique in awe. "Does Devin know what you are doing?"

"Somebody has to look out for him," Abbey said. She unzipped the backpack and gave him the thumb drive. "Picture number 13278 is what you are looking for."

Victor took the information from Abbey. He gave her a quick hug. "Again Abbey, I am sorry for your loss."

"I should have listened to you," Abbey began. "I never—"

"Abbey, what happened was not your fault," Victor said.

"That doesn't help Ricky, does it?"

Victor shook his head. "No. It doesn't."

"I'm going to bed now," Abbey said.

Without another word, Victor and Dominique left the room.

"Poor thing," Dominique said, closing the door behind her. She trailed Victor down the stairs.

"She just gave us some extremely helpful information," Victor said. He headed into the private study. He was anxious to review the information.

"Are you going to do that now?" Dominique glanced at the clock on the wall. "It's 2:15 in the morning. You need to get some rest. You have been at it all day."

Victor tried to put the thumb drive into the desk top computer. Dominique quickly grabbed it from his hand.

"Give it back to me," Victor ordered.

"Oh no, that is enough for you today."

"I have not been this close," Victor argued. "I want to see what is on that thumb drive."

"That same information will be there an hour or two from now," she scolded. "You need to get some sleep. You don't have to worry about being on stakeout because everyone is here. I turned the alarm on. This place is safe." She gestured to him with a finger. "Let's go, Colonel. Time for bed."

***

The next morning, Victor flipped over to find that he was in bed alone. Dominique was gone. The early morning sunlight streaming through the bedroom window hit him in the face. It's been months since he had been in his Gaithersburg home. The FOR SALE sign was still in the front yard. He'd been unable to get rid of it. With everything that is going on, it was for the best.

Victor looked over at the bedside clock. It was 8:00 a.m. He managed to get about five hours of sleep. He had to admit that he felt rested. He swung his legs over the side of the king size bed. The smell of bacon, eggs, and French toast tickled his nose. His stomach growled. He realized that it has been hours since he had anything to eat.

He made his way into the adjoining bathroom, took a quick shower, and brushed his teeth. He managed to find some clothing in the closet.

He made his way downstairs to find that everyone involved in the case was sitting at the dining room table. They were chatting and having breakfast.

"Good morning, boss," Paul spoke.

The room went quiet a moment.

"Good morning everyone," Victor said. He buttoned his shirt and pushed the sleeves up. "I see everyone is here."

"Tonya is on her way," Dominique said. She poured Dani another glass of orange juice. She pointed to the chair at the table for Victor. "Have a seat. Your French toast is getting cold."

Victor looked around the table. "Where's Abbey?"

"I'm here," the small voice said from the top of the stairs. She made her way into the dining room. She sat next to Maya who reached out and patted her on the back in comfort.

"How did you sleep?" Dominique asked.

"Not very well," Abbey said.

"Detective West will be here to speak with you around ten." Victor settled in the chair.

"I'm sorry to hear about your loss," Dani said.

"Thank you," Abbey said.

"Dominique said he was your boyfriend," Dani continued.

"Yes. Two years," Abbey answered.

"That's a long time," Dominique said.

Everyone nodded.

"Dani, have you ever been to the Red Door?" Victor asked out of the blue. He shoved a fork of French toast in his mouth.

"The Red Door? The Red Door?" Dani said aloud. She drew her perfect arched eyebrow together. "No. It's a dive. Not exactly my kind of crowd if you know what I mean. Why do you ask?"

"The bartender, Luis Orchard, says that he remembers you coming into the club on the night of the murder."

Dani's fork slipped out of her hand. "What? What time?"

"We don't know yet. That's what we are going to find out," Paul said. "Boss, I would like to have another talk with Mr. Luis Orchard."

"I thought you said that you didn't get anywhere the first time," Victor said.

"I didn't," Paul said. "I would like to speak with him again."

Victor smirked. "Will this time be any different?"

"Damn right," Paul said without hesitation.

"Paul?" Victor prompted.

"I'm not going to hurt him."

"I hope not," Victor said. "Maybe someone should go with you."

"Colonel," Paul said.

A knock and then Tonya's head appeared in the kitchen door. She smiled at the scene. "Wow this is different."

Gerald brought up the rear. "Full house. Any room at the table for a starving man?"

"You can have my spot," Victor said. "I need to do some work in the study."

"You barely touched your food," Dominique scolded. "Take it with you."

Victor picked up the plate of food. He hurried into the library.

"I'll go with you," Paul said, grabbing a piece of toast. He stuffed it in his mouth and followed Victor.

Victor walked behind the desk and plugged the thumb drive into the USB port. Paul pulled up a chair. "I had an interesting talk with Abbey last night," he began.

"How so?"

"She told me that her boss didn't keep records of the shop transactions for obvious reasons, but she did." Victor typed through a serious of screens. "On the day Priest came into the shop, she managed to get a license plate number and address from a car rental agency that he used. It was a silver Ford Escape. SUV."

"A second vehicle?" Paul asked.

"I'm sure he didn't give them a correct name and address," Victor said. "He is two steps ahead of us. I don't like it. This time, I want to be the one that surprises him."

Victor looked up to see Gerald coming into the study. He was sipping a glass of orange juice.

"What's going on, fellas?" Gerald asked.

"Trying to get an address," Victor said. "Priest rented a car." He hit the ENTER key. The screen opened. "Okay. Image 13278 is the receipt we are looking for."

"There it is." Paul pointed to the screen.

"John Franklin Davis," Victor began. "Sounds fake already." He chuckled. "John Franklin Davis. 1378 Cannon Ball Road. Driver License number W-530-668-186-002."

"Sounds like a long shot," Paul said.

"Not necessarily," Gerald said. He rushed over to shoo Victor from the chair. "Let me have a crack at it."

"What are you going to do?" Victor asked.

"Gerald is very good at what he's about to do," Tonya said, coming into the room. She grinned and nodded at her brother.

"What he's about to do?" Victor asked in an inquisitive tone. He looked from Tonya to Gerald. His fingers were expertly flying over the computer keys.

"There really is a John Franklin Davis. Several of them." He continued typing. "One is five years old. Too young. One is forty-two. African-American. The other is seventy-nine years old. White. He lives in District Heights, Maryland. I will go with the latter."

"There are a lot of Warehouses in that area," Tonya added.

Gerald continued typing. Victor walked over and looked over his brother's shoulder. He was surprised when he saw a schematic screen with an aerial view of the local streets and houses. "There is no 1378 Canon Ball but there is a 7831 Canon Ball Road. Mr. Davis, the seventy-nine-year old, lives on that street." He minimized the screen and quickly logged into the Police Department database.

Victor was floored. "Gerald?"

"I just want to check something out," Gerald said with confidence. He continued typing. "Just as I thought, Mr. Davis reported his wallet stolen."

"Before or after the murder?" Tonya asked.

"It was before," Gerald answered.

"Sounds like he stole the information, changed it just a little, and rented a car," Tonya said.

"More than likely," Paul said. "He drove that vehicle to kill Sterling."

"You get the prize," Gerald said. "He returned the vehicle the next day." He logged off the computer.

"All of that is great," Victor said. "We still don't know where to find Priest."

"Sure, you do," Gerald said. "I just told you."

Victor frowned. "How do you figure that?"

"Where does Mr. Davis live?" Tonya reminded him.

Victor tilted his head. He thought a moment and snapped his fingers. "The Warehouse District."

"This guy has a hard one for warehouses," Paul said.

"The area is not as big as the Wharf," Victor said. "If I'm lucky, I'll find the white Pontiac."

"It's probably where he lives," Paul said. "I know a lot of homeless people hang around that area. Good place to disappear. No one looks for you there."

Victor glanced at Gerald. He didn't know what to say. He never knew his brother had those types of skills. "We will definitely talk later."

"You're welcome. You know where to find me." Gerald headed for the door.

"Gerald." Paul called behind him. "Tell me about Luis Orchard." He placed a hand on his shoulder as they left the room.

"You could have been a little bit more grateful," Tonya said. "He just handed you a big break."

"How long has he been a hacker?" Victor asked.

Tonya made a face. "Since college."

Victor leaned back. "Since college. You have got to be kidding me."

Tonya shook her head. "No."

"Did Dad know?" Victor asked.

"You remember that time Gerald was suspended from college for a semester?" Tonya replied.

"Yeah. Dad said a college prank went wrong."

"It did," Tonya said. "Gerald hacked into the school computer. He got caught changing the grade for the star of the basketball team."

"You can be kicked out of school for that."

"Dad worked his magic. It was the star of the team," Tonya said. "That player is now in the NBA."

"Unbelievable," Victor said. "He hasn't done anything illegal lately that you know of, has he?"

Tonya shook her head. "No. He promised Dad that he wouldn't get into any more trouble. He kept that promise. He only did that to help you. He wants your agency to be successful."

Victor ran a hand down the front of his face. "How good is he?"

"Gerald is a computer wizard," Tonya said.

"I'm speechless," Victor said. "I spoke with Dominique last night." He changed the subject.

"She told me that you caught the son and stepmother together."

"I did," Tonya said. "Very intense chemistry between those two. I'm sure she told you that he gave her a very expensive bracelet."

"Like I told Dominique, it doesn't mean a thing if you can't tie one or both of them to the killer."

"I know that," Tonya said. "It's still disgusting. They didn't even try to hide it. I was too embarrassed to ask them about it."

"Why should they hide it?" Victor asked. "Old man Sterling is dead. They don't have to hide anymore."

"What about decency?" Tonya asked.

Victor chuckled. "If they had any, they wouldn't be having an affair in the first place. That family doesn't even know the meaning of the word."

"I'm telling you, they did it," Tonya said. "I just know it."

Victor shook his head. "I know how it looks. You want to believe that because you disapprove of what they are doing."

"I believe that because I think those two conspired to have old man Sterling killed."

"No. It's too tidy. Too neat."

"The preliminary hearing is at the end of the week," Tonya reminded him. "It will give me a chance to see what the prosecution has, but I do not want to go to trial."

"I'm aware of that," Victor said in a sincere tone. "What the prosecution have is circumstantial. I believe we can refute that. I told you about Priest."

"He sounds like a real piece of work," Tonya said.

"You don't want to meet him in a dark alley," Victor said. "Also, I'm sure Gerald told you about the bartender from the Red Door."

"Yes. He told me," Tonya said. "That is a big break. Let's hope Paul will have better luck this time."

"I'm hoping the search at the warehouse will also bear fruit," Victor said. "How are things going with Stephen?" He changed the subject again

Tonya shrugged. "Stephen will be Stephen."

"What does that mean?"

"Just that he has his way of thinking," Tonya said. "I have mine."

"Tonya—" Victor tried to interject.

"I already told you that I wasn't going to turn my back on a friend," Tonya said.

"Are you guys talking about it?" Victor asked.

"If that's what you want to call it." Tonya walked around the desk. She began removing files from her brief case.

"Stephen hasn't come around?" Victor asked.

"I don't expect him to," Tonya said. "I knew what kind of man he was when I married him. At the time, I thought I wanted that, too."

"And now?" Victor asked.

"It's not enough," Tonya said. "Taking this case, I realize that I want it all. I want to be a wife, mother, and a damn good criminal attorney."

"If Stephen doesn't come around, what then?" Victor asked.

Tonya sat in the large, black leather chair. She let out a small sigh. "I don't know, Victor. I don't know."

"I hope you never have to find out," Victor said.

"Neither do I," Tonya said.

A few minutes later, Victor called everyone into the study. He filled them in on everything about the case so far. He pulled Abbey, Tonya, and Paul to the side to inform them of the decision to tell the media that Abbey was the victim.

"I'm on my way to see the bartender." Paul said. He walked toward the door.

"Hold on. I'm coming with you," Maya said. She was hot on his trail.

"What? Why?" Paul asked.

"You're going to need my help," Maya replied.

"I'm more than capable of talking with Mr. Orchard." Paul said. "I don't need your help."

"I know where the Red Door is. If I don't go with you, I'll just go on my own," Maya argued.

"You know she will," Tonya added.

"You might as well let her go with you," Dani threw in. "I know my sister, she will speak with the bartender with or without you."

Paul glanced at Victor. He shrugged. "It's up to you."

"Alright," Paul reluctantly gave in. He turned and headed toward the door. "When we get there just follow my lead." He said over his right shoulder, "I will check in later."

"What are the chances of her listening to Paul?" Tonya asked.

"Slim to none," Victor replied as he watched the dynamic duo walk out the door.

Chapter Ten

"Why are we back at the Red Door?" Maya asked. "We are back where we started a couple of hours ago," she said when Paul parked in front of the club.

"That right," Paul replied. "We started out here. The club was closed earlier. We went to his home and he wasn't there either and now we are back."

"There better be a good reason why we are here again," Maya said, looking around.

"Luis is here," Paul said.

"How do you know?"

Paul pointed to the black Jeep Wrangler at the end of the lot. "That's his truck." He exited the car. "Remember, let me ask the questions."

"I know," Maya said, following in step with Paul.

Paul pulled the glass double door open. He stepped inside to the sound of soft rock music pumping through the speakers. A couple of employees were scurrying around cleaning the main area.

A red-headed young woman that looked to be in her early twenties stepped in front of Paul. She placed the tray of glasses on a table. Dressed in a pair of blue denim shorts, a tight white tee-shirt, and short black boots. She looked him up and down. "We're not opened yet."

"That's okay," Paul said. "I'm looking for Luis Orchard."

"What do you want with him?" the woman said.

"I need to talk with him"

The woman straightened. "About what?"

"That's personal," Paul answered. "Is he here?"

"We need to talk to him about the Montgomery Sterling murder," Maya volunteered.

"He doesn't know anything," the woman said.

"How would you know?" Paul asked.

"I'm his woman. I know everything," she said. "I know he's saying that Dani McCall was here on the night of the murder."

Maya became irritated. "What are you saying? My sister wasn't here."

The woman half-chuckled. "Your sister?"

"That's right. My sister," Maya quipped. "What of it?"

"You're Dani McCall sister?" the male voice said, walking casually toward them. Black, curly hair almost fully covered a handsome face. Piercing blue eyes, set charmingly within their sockets, smiled at them. Dark stubble delightfully compliments his hair and cheekbones.

Paul recognized Luis Orchard. He seemed pleased to meet with him. The last time he wouldn't give him the time of day.

"It's good to see you again," Luis said, extending a hand.

"The last time you were not happy to see me." Paul accepted his handshake.

"That was before I found out that you work for Gerald's brother," Luis said. "I didn't want to get involved."

"Regardless of who Paul works for," Maya said, "you should want to help if you can."

"It's not always that easy," Luis said. He guided them to a table. He refocused on his girlfriend. "It's okay, Lizzy. I need to talk to these guys."

Lizzy gave them a look. She picked up the tray and walked to the back of the club. He sat across from Paul. "Don't mind Lizzy. She means well."

"I understand." Paul took out his cell. "I hope you don't mind. I'm recording your statement."

Luis waved a hand in midair. "I don't mind. I don't know if what I have to say will help Ms. McCall."

"You said my sister was here the night of the murder?" Maya said.

Paul gave Maya a look. "We agreed that I would ask the questions."

"Sorry," Maya said.

"You told Gerald that Dani McCall was here on the night of the murder," Paul said. "Do you remember the time?"

"She came in around eleven that night," Luis said.

Maya's face beamed with excitement. "This cleared my sister."

"Not really," Paul said. He refocused on Luis. "How can you be so sure about the time?"

"I was leaving at eleven-thirty," Louis said. "She came in before I left for the night. Lizzy and I drove to New York the next morning to see her parents. I got off early so that I could beat the early morning traffic. I recognized Dani McCall. She's my favorite new anchor. It was her. I'm sure of it."

"You saw her come in," Paul said. "But you didn't see her leave?"

"No," Luis answered. "I can only vouch for the time she came in." He pointed to the front of the club. "When I left, she was sitting at the end of the bar, drinking."

"Did she look drunk to you?" Paul asked.

"I can't say," Luis said. "I didn't get close enough to make a judgement. But I can tell you that if a customer looks like they had too much to drink, we cut them off."

Paul glanced around the club. "Do you have cameras in or outside the club?"

Luis chuckled. "No. No cameras. The closest camera is at the light on the corner."

"Thanks," Paul said.

"I wish I could be more help to Ms. McCall," Luis said.

"You have helped more than you think." Paul stood.

"I hope things work out for Ms. McCall," Louis said. "Like I said, I'm one of her biggest fans. To be honest, I'm surprised no one else has come forward. I can't believe that I'm the only one that saw her that night."

"I can't believe it either," Maya said.

"Let's go," Paul said to Maya. He extended a hand to Luis. "Thanks. I appreciate it."

"No problem," Luis said, accepting the handshake.

"What we just learned wasn't good for my sister, was it?" Maya said, standing in front of the bar.

Paul pointed the fob at the vehicle to disarm it. "What we know for sure is that Dani left Cadence around nine o'clock p.m. She didn't make it to the Red Door until eleven p.m."

Maya rolled her eyes in irritation. "There's a two-hour gap."

"Exactly," Paul said. "She had plenty of time to commit the murder or have someone do it for her."

***

Victor wandered in and out of several warehouses. So far there was no sign of Priest. He looked to see a middle-aged woman pushing a loaded cart from one side of the street to the other. Though the heat was in the mid-eighties, she was wearing polka dot galoshes, a pink rain jacket, and a red scarf on her head.

"Excuse me," Victim said.

The woman threw her arms up in defense as if Victor was going to strike her.

140

"Don't be afraid," he assured her. "I was just going to ask if you live around here."

The woman's face softened. "You scared me half to death. I live here. There. I live everywhere. What do you want?"

"I'm looking for someone," Victor said. "I thought you may have seen him."

"Twenty dollars," the woman said.

Victor chuckled. "You don't even know who I'm looking for."

"Whether I have seen him or not, you are taking up my time," the woman said. "That is going to cost you." She eyed Victor up and down. She removed the scarf and ran her hand through her salt-and-pepper hair. "Just because I look like this doesn't mean my time isn't valuable. It looks like you have it to spare."

Victor reached into his back pocket for his wallet. He removed a twenty. The woman's eyes grew large as saucers at the sight of the money. She reached for it. He drew his hand back. "Not so fast. Can I tell you whom I'm looking for?"

She nodded her head.

"I'm looking for a man about forty. Receding hair line. White, about five-feet ten-inches or eleven. Medium build."

The woman flashed Victor a blank look.

"Driving a white Pontiac," Victor heard a male voice say. He looked to see a young black man walking toward them. He was dressed in military khakis, carrying a duffle bag over his shoulder.

"Exactly," Victor answered. "Have you seen him?"

"Stay out of this, Chuck!" the woman yelled. "This is my money."

The man nodded. "The old woman means well but she doesn't know anything."

"You do?"

"I know where the man is that you are looking for," the man answered.

"Where can I find him?" Victor asked.

"The off-white split-level warehouse at the end of the street." The man pointed. "He's been there all week. Keeps to himself. He just came back in about ten minutes ago." He turned to leave.

"Don't you want the twenty?"

"No," the young man said over his shoulders. "I don't need a handout. I prefer to work for my money." He began walking away again.

"What kind of work?"

The man turned around. "Since I've left the military, I've done all kinds of odd jobs. I've worked as a dish washer to construction."

"I'm part owner of a supper club." Victor reached in his wallet. He removed a business card. "If you are serious about looking for work, stop by. Give them this card."

The man accepted the card. A slight smile crossed the man's face. "I'll stop by." He walked off without another word.

"What about me?" the woman snapped.

Victor handed her the twenty. He continued toward the building. He pulled out his cell phone and made a call to Detective West. He was on another assignment. He left the address of where he was and left instructions for him to meet him as soon as possible.

The warehouse looked deserted. It had seen better days and needed a paint job. Half of the windows on the top floor were broken out and were boarded up. He was looking for a way in without being seen. He quickly moved to the left side of the building. He found himself standing underneath a large window. He stood on his tiptoes and peeped inside.

He spotted Priest walking around a spacious, empty room. He was talking on his cell phone. From his facial expressions, he appeared to be in a heated argument with someone. "There has to be a way in," he said to himself.

Victor looked around for a back or side door. He was about to give up when he looked past Priest. He spotted a damaged large exit sign. It was barely hanging above a door. That would be his way in. Next to it was an empty office enclosed in glass. The Pontiac was parked alongside of it. From what he could see, Priest was able to drive in and out of the back of the warehouse without being detected. It would explain why the vehicle was never seen.

Victor made his way around back to the other side of the warehouse. He tried the door. It was locked. He would have to pick it. He reached in his pocket. He slid the knife down on top of the lock bolt, applied some pressure, and in no time popped the lock.

Victor carefully crept inside. He hid behind the wall. He peeped in the office to see Priest inside. He was still on the phone. His feet were propped on the desk.

"I want the rest of my money, now!" Priest was saying. "You heard on the news that woman is dead. Do you think the cops care about that?"

Victor moved behind the door. He crouched under the glass partition to hear better.

"Don't even think about not paying me," Priest quipped. "You know what I am capable of."

Victor took out his phone to record the conversation, when he accidently stepped on a coke can, the noise caused Priest to look around. He ended the call and jumped to his feet.

With the quickness of a cat, Victor moved with ease to the other side of the office. He crawled alongside the parked vehicle inside the large spacious room.

A moment later, Victor watched as Priest got in the vehicle. He made a beeline to the other side of the room.

Priest turned on the ignition, threw the car in drive, and drove out threw the wall of the warehouse.

Victor ran after him as he was speeding recklessly down the street. He chased him to the end of the block only to see him make a 360 degree turn back toward him. Victor ran as fast as his legs could take him in the opposite direction. He peeped over his left shoulder to see that the car was hot on his trail. The window was down and a .357 appeared. He rolled out of the way just as two shots rang out over his head.

This time the vehicle sped to the end of the street. It made a fast left at the Stop sign and disappeared. It slowed down just enough for him to get a license plate number.

"You won't get away this time," Victor said out loud. He brushed the dirt off his pants, then placed his hand on his hips. He made his way back into the warehouse.

Victor hurried back into the office. There were papers scattered over the top of the desk. "There has to be something here on who hired him," he said to himself. He began to go through the papers. His eyes scanned every document. There was nothing until he got to the last sheet.

He pulled out his phone and made a video call to Tonya.

"Where are you?" Tonya asked.

"I'm at what use to be Priest's place."

"Are you okay?" Tonya asked. "You look pissed."

"I was almost road kill and he shot at me," Victor said. "So, you can say I'm a little pissed."

"Did you find out who hired Priest?"

"I have an idea. I need to follow up on what I found," Victor said. "I'm taking photos and sending them to you. You can look them over. Anything from Paul and Maya?"

"It's not good." Tonya filled Victor in on what Paul found out.

"Two-hour gap," Victor said.

"We need to get the video footage from the camera," Tonya said.

"We can get it, but it won't help much," Victor said. "The prosecution will just argue what we already know, that a hitman was hired. Except they think Dani hired him."

"I'll get Gerald to pull it for us," Tonya said. "The evidence is good to have."

"I agree. Have faith little sister," Victor said. "It may look bad, but everything may not be what it seems. I just found what I believe is a smoking gun. It's good news for Dani. We will talk later." Victor ended the video call.

A moment later, the sound of sirens could be heard in the background. It was the second time in the past twelve hours. He was getting used to it.

"I received your message, I got here as quick as I could," Detective West said, walking toward him. He looked at the large hole in the side of the warehouse. "What happened here?"

"A vehicle drove through it," Victor joked.

"I can see that," Detective West quipped. "Whose vehicle?"

Victor ignored the question. "I need you to put out an APB for license plate 2C0879."

"Who does the plate number belong to?"

"Priest," Victor answered. "This is where he was hiding out."

Detective West instructed his men to search the warehouse. "Where are you headed?"

"Back to my office," Victor said. "Call me on my cell," Victor replied as he headed to his vehicle.

"What did you find out?" Detective West asked.

Victor didn't respond.

"This is not how this is supposed to work," Detective West said after him.

***

"Priest got away from you again?" Tonya teased. She walked into what will be her office.

Victor bought up the rear. He looked around the room bustling with people coming and going. "What's going on?"

"I told you the computers and phones will be installed today," Dominique said, walking into the office. "They are just finishing up. How soon they forget."

"I'm only working on a murder case," Victor said. He refocused on Tonya. "This time, I managed to get a license plate number. I put out an APB. He will pop up again. I will be ready. Did you look over the information I sent you? You may have been right about Spencer Montgomery. He owed a lot of money to a bookie."

"About two-hundred-fifty-thousands-dollar worth," Tonya said. "Get rid of the old man and he will have all of his old man money."

"And his wife," Victor added.

"I told you Spencer was guilty," Dominque said with satisfaction.

"You're still not convinced," Tonya said to Victor.

"As I said before, it's too neat," Victor said. "My gut keeps telling me something is missing."

"But I'm looking at the evidence that you gave me," Tonya argued.

Victor paced back and forth in front of the desk. He always trusted his gut instinct. Right now, his gut was telling him that something wasn't adding up. He had to find Priest. He was the only one that could give him the answers he was looking for.

"I heard you found something at Priest's hideout," Dani said, standing in the doorway.

146

"What are you doing here?" Victor said. "You're supposed to be at the hideout." He looked over her shoulders. He spotted Maya with pen and notepad in hand. "Maya?"

"Maya will be your Receptionist?" Dominique said. "I hired her. I hope you don't mind."

"I don't," Victor said. He focused on Dani. "I did find something at Priest's. It looks like Spencer owes a bookie a lot of money."

"There were rumors that Spencer likes to play the horses," Dani said.

"Tell me more," Victor said.

"Folks were saying that his father bailed him out more than once," Dani said. "He was tired of paying off his debts and cut him off."

That could make things tense between father and son," Tonya said.

Victor held up a piece of paper. "This confirms that."

"Tonya told you what we found out at the Red Door?" Paul asked, waltzing in the office.

"There's a two-hour gap," Victor said. He looked at Dani. "You have had a couple of days to think. Have you remembered anything about that night?"

"I've tried," Dani said. "Nothing. I don't even remember how I got home from the Red Door."

"It was a Lyft," Gerald said from the doorway. "I managed to look at the CCTV pictures from the camera on the corner. The Bouncers were nice enough to put you in it. The time was eleven-nineteen p.m."

Dani lowered her head. "Oh my god. How embarrassing."

"At least you got home safely," Tonya said.

"I blacked out," Dani said. "It happens every time I drink."

"Is that going to be your defense?" the female voice said behind Gerald said.

All heads turned to find D.A. Stephanie Bigelow standing in the door. Dressed in a tan two-piece skirt suit with a ruffle bottom, Stephanie strolled further in the room. She tossed the

expensive, brown, silk scarf around her neck. Matching two-inch stilettos were on her feet. Her makeup was flawless, not a hair was out of place, and she looked like she stepped off the pages of vogue.

"Stephanie Bigelow?" Tonya said, coming to her feet. "What are you doing here?"

"The question should be how did she find us?" Gerald asked. He stepped aside to let Stephanie enter the room.

Stephanie looked around the room. "I see everyone I heard about is here." She nodded at Victor. "Mr. Sexton." She tossed her shoulder length, blonde hair over her shoulder.

"What can I do for you, Ms. Bigelow?" Victor asked.

"I came to have a word with Mrs. Sims," Stephanie said.

"About me?" Dani said.

"Of course," Stephanie said. "Can we have a moment?"

"I don't see why not," Tonya said. "Okay guys, let us have a moment." She pointed to the empty seat across from the desk. "Stephanie, have a seat. Excuse the mess. We are still getting settled in."

Stephanie took a seat. She crossed one long leg over the other. "It's okay. I'm glad to see you are back practicing criminal law. I miss my favorite sparring partner."

"I'll let you ladies talk," Victor said.

"No. Victor why don't you stay?" Tonya said. She focused on Stephanie. "Stephanie, you don't mind if my brother stays, do you?"

"Not at all." Stephanie smiled at Victor. "I have heard a lot about Mr. Sexton. Your reputation precedes you."

"Thank you," Victor said. "I think."

"Don't worry," Stephanie said. "It was good reviews."

"I wasn't worried," Victor said. "What brings you to VSI?"

"I wanted to talk to you about your client," Stephanie said. "We have her dead to right. We have the murder weapon; ballistics results confirm it. We also have a room full of witnesses that overheard Ms. McCall threaten to kill him."

"It doesn't mean that Ms. McCall killed him," Victor said. "What's her motive?"

Stephanie chuckled. She pointed at Victor. "Good way to find out what we know." She stood. "We also know that Mr. Sterling suspended Ms. McCall a week without pay and put her assistant in the anchor chair. We have her dead to right. It's premediated murder."

"That's nonsense," Tonya said.

"Why are you here, Ms. Bigelow?" Victor asked.

"If your client pleads guilty," Stephanie said. "We will take life in prison off the table."

"Then what?" Tonya said. "You will ask the judge for twenty-five to life."

"That's exactly what Ms. Bigelow is seeking," Victor said.

"It's better than life," Stephanie said.

"Just out of curiosity," Victor said. "Are you looking at anyone else to be the killer?"

"The other suspects we looked at all have alibis," Stephanie boasted. She looked out the window. "Nice view," she said.

"In other words, you're not looking at anyone besides Ms. McCall," Victor said.

"There's no need too," Stephanie said.

"We will have to deny your plea deal," Tonya said.

"I know you have not practiced criminal law for a while," Stephanie said. "This is a great deal. I would take it, if I were you."

Tonya stood. "No, thank you. If you are so sure about Dani McCall, then you will have to prove it at the preliminary hearing. I think what you have is all circumstantial."

"You can prove that?" Stephanie asked.

"I wouldn't say it if I couldn't prove it," Tonya said. "This case is not going to trial."

Stephanie chuckled. "Not going to trial. That's a good one." She leaned down to pick up her briefcase. "I will see you at the hearing."

"Yes, you will," Tonya said.

"It was nice meeting you, Mr. Sexton," Stephanie said. She turned on her heels and walked out the door.

"I see what you mean," Victor said. "Barracuda fits her."

"I have to choose between the two of you," Tonya said, "my money is on you. So, get out there and find Priest."

Chapter Eleven

"Are you ready?" Dominique asked Tonya a couple of days later as she dressed for court.

"Ready as I will ever be." Tonya ran a hand over her navy-blue skirt suit. "How do I look?" She turned around to check her appearance in the floor length mirror.

"You not only look professional, but you look fierce," Dominique said. "That's what you want today, to look fierce."

Tonya snapped her fingers. "That's right, fierce. Have you heard anything from Victor or Paul?" she asked, wrapping an expensive scarf around her neck.

"Last I heard they were on stakeouts. Nothing from either one of them," Dominique said. "Don't worry."

"What do you mean, don't worry?" Tonya said.

"Morning, Mommy," her son, Liam, said from the doorway. He came further in the room, struggling to carry her briefcase.

"Oh, come here baby," Tonya cooed. "What do you have there?"

"I bought your case. Good luck, Mommy. I'll be cheering for you."

Tonya reached out, running her hand over his short haircut. She gave him a tight hug and followed it with a kiss on the top of the head.

"Mom!" Liam whined.

"I can't help it," Tonya said. "You are so cute, missing front tooth and all." She took the case from him. She glanced at her watch. "We better get going." She took

Liam's hand, leading him down the stairs. "I'm glad you're my assistant today," she said over her left shoulder to Dominique. "If you weren't here, I don't know what I would do."

"Are you kidding?" Dominique teased. "I wouldn't have it any other way. I'm looking forward to this case. I'll just fill in until you hire someone permanently."

"I never thought about it," Tonya said. "I guess I will have to hire someone."

"Well, think about it."

Tonya looked over to Stephen. He was in the study going over some drawings. He never looked in her direction. "I'm leaving, Stephen," she called, grabbing her purse off the coat rack. Her husband did not respond. Glancing at him for a moment, she slowly walked out the door.

"Maybe he didn't hear you," Dominique said.

"He heard me," Tonya said.

They looked to find Dani and Maya waiting by Tonya's vehicle.

"You look nice," Tonya called.

"So, do you," Dani threw back.

"Are you ready?" Tonya asked. "This is it."

"Do I have a choice?" Dani asked. "I feel good about today."

Tonya tapped her on the shoulder. "Good. Keep that feeling. Let's do this."

***

"Detective West, after the arresting officer found the murder weapon under the seat of the defendant's car, what did you do?" Prosecutor Stephanie Bigelow asked.

"I sent it to the lab for a ballistic check," Detective West replied.

"What did you find?" the prosecutor asked.

"We found that we had a perfect match," Detective West answered. "The gun was used to shoot and kill Sterling Montgomery."

"Thank you, Detective West," Stephanie said. "I reserve the right to call this witness again," she said to the court.

"Mrs. Sims," Judge Manson Munford said, "do you have questions for Detective West?"

Tonya was so absorbed in looking over her notes, she almost jumped out of her skin. Her palms were sweating, and her heart was beating a mile a minute. "Calm down," she said to herself. "Just like riding a horse. Dani is depending on you." She glanced over at Dani. She gave her a reassuring smile.

Tonya closed the folder. She walked confidently toward Detective West still on the witness stand.

He nodded.

"Detective West," Tonya began. "How many times was the deceased shot?"

"Two times, Mrs. Sims."

"How close were the points of entry of the bullets?" Tonya asked. "Now before you answer and with the court's permission. I would like my assistant to stand approximately the same distance as the killer."

Dominique cocked an eyebrow.

"The court has no problem with the demonstration," Judge Munford replied.

Tonya motioned for Dominique to head to the back of the court room. "Ms. Frazier will be Mr. Sterling. You will be the killer. For court purposes only."

The courtroom chuckled.

"Now, Detective West," Tonya said. "I will repeat my last question. How close were the two entry points?"

"The two shots all came within a diameter of an inch of the injury."

"That's about the size of a silver dollar." Tonya pulled a coin from her suit coat pocket. She handed it to the Detective to examine. "That's quite a shot. You're a trained marksman, Detective. Could you make that shot?"

Detective West examined the coin. "Are you kidding? Not even on my best day."

"The shot would have to be fired simultaneously, am I right?" Tonya asked.

Detective West nodded in agreement. "That is correct."

"I mean if the victim moved, turned, or even fell, then one of the targets would have changed, am I right?"

"That is also correct?"

"Could you get off two rounds that quickly, Detective?"

"Probably not, Mrs. Sims," Detective West explained. "But then I was never a professional athlete. In college, Ms. McCall excelled in archery. She has good hand skills, vision, and reflexes."

"Objection, Your Honor," Tonya said.

"Detective West just answer the questions put to you," Judge Munford scolded.

"Yes, Your Honor," Detective West said.

"It was over fifteen years ago that Dani McCall was a professional athlete," Tonya said. "You just mentioned the defendant's physical capabilities. Thank you for that. Doctor Nugent, can you please stand?"

A middle-aged, dark-haired woman stood. "Dr. Nugent treated the defendant for several years while she was in and out of college. She is ready to testify that she injured her right hand and later it became arthritic, leaving her trigger finger with limited mobility. If that is the case, how can Dani McCall fire that quickly to hit the victim as he moved?"

"Objection, Your Honor," Stephanie said. "That's speculation."

"Nonsense, Your Honor," Tonya said. "Detective West has investigated hundreds of shootings."

"Something like that," Detective West answered.

"I think Detective West is more than qualified to answer the question," Tonya said. "I would consider him an expert witness."

"I will allow it," Judge Munford said.

"Thank you, your Honor." Tonya's face brightened. "Detective West, as an expert witness, can a shooter with an arthritic condition and impaired mobility to their trigger finger fire three shots quickly enough to have hit the target?" She pointed toward Dominique still standing at the back of the court room.

Detective West wiggled in his seat. "I doubt it," he finally answered.

Tonya gave Dani a slight smile. She scored a major point. "Thank you, Detective West." She made her way back to the counselor's table. "No more questions."

"Redirect?" Judge Munford asked.

"Yes, there is," Stephanie said. "Detective West is there any reason the defendant couldn't have fired the weapon with her left hand?"

"Objection!" Tonya called. "Cause for speculation." *Good one*, she said to herself. She flashed Stephanie a fake smile.

"I will allow it, Mrs. Sims. Fair is fair."

"The defendant could have used her left hand," Detective West said.

"What about accuracy?" Stephanie asked, proud of herself as she glanced over at the defendant's table.

"Well, with the distance in question, how steady the hands are, and with good eye sight, an athlete like Ms. McCall once was, she could easily have used her left hand."

"Hypothetical," Tonya called.

Stephanie tilted her blonde head to one side. She flashed Tonya a fake smile. "Of course." She strolled back to her table.

"Re-cross?" Judge Munford asked Tonya.

"No re-cross," Tonya answered.

"You may step down," Judge Munford instructed Detective West. "Ms. Bigelow?"

"The People rest," Stephanie said.

"Mrs. Sims is the defense prepared to call its first witness?" Judge Munford asked.

"Yes, Your Honor," Tonya answered. "The defense calls Ginger Fox."

Ginger Fox rose from the middle of the courtroom with her head held-high. She was dressed in a stunning, expensive white dress. A large brim hat and matching pumps completed the ensemble. She strolled to the front of the courtroom. She made herself comfortable on the witness stand and crossed one leg over the other.

Tonya couldn't wait to cross examine Ginger Fox. "Mrs. Fox, will you please tell the court how well you knew the deceased?"

Ginger tried to put on a brave face, but Tonya could tell she was nervous. "I worked for the station as a news anchor, and we were also in business together. He knew I was very much into women's issues and we talked about working together on a Domestic Abuse project."

"That particular project was scrapped, wasn't it?"

Ginger nodded. "Yes."

"We found out that Sterling Montgomery likes to fool around," Tonya said. "Word is he was seeing someone. Can you tell us who it was?"

Ginger blinked. "How would I know something like that?"

"Because you two worked very closely together," Tonya said. "We also heard Sterling Montgomery was thinking of getting married again, so I'll ask you again, can you tell us who he was seeing?"

"Well, he did hit on me from time to time," Ginger said. "But that was his nature. I never took him serious."

"But Mr. Montgomery was a very serious man," Tonya said. "He even spoke to his attorney about divorcing his wife."

"He told me the same thing," Ginger said. "He said that he put me in his Will. But like I said, I didn't take him seriously."

Tonya looked out in the courtroom to find Paula and Spencer sitting next to each other in the second row. The looks on their faces said it all; they were flabbergasted. "A new Will? Then shortly after that, he broke things off and then several weeks later your women project was scrapped. Isn't that true?"

Ginger straightened. "No, that's not true."

"Oh, come on now," Tonya said. "Isn't it true that you were personally and professionally betrayed by Sterling Spencer? When you asked to be compensated for his betrayal, he refused and fired you."

A look of panic washed across Ginger's face. "I learned the hard way what Sterling Spencer was like, but I didn't kill him. Besides, I'm the one that broke things off and I definitely wasn't going to marry him."

"Oh, come on now. Spencer Sterling is one of the richest men in the country. He owns one of the prestigious news stations in the most powerful cities in the world, and you expect us to believe that you did not want to marry him?"

"That is exactly what I'm telling you," Ginger answered with attitude.

"So, why don't you enlighten us to the reason you turned him down?" Tonya said.

"Because, I'm already married."

"You're married to your attorney?"

"Yes. I have been married for five years," Ginger said. "When I was seeing Spencer, we were separated. I'm not proud of what I did, but we managed to work things out."

Tonya thought of Stephen. She hoped they would also be able to work on their marriage. "No more questions."

"Ms. Bigelow?" Judge Munford asked.

"No questions at this time, Your Honor." Stephanie said.

"The witness is excused," Judge Munford said. "It is coming up on the lunch hour. Court will resume again at one o'clock." He hit the gavel.

Tonya noticed the glance given between Paula and Ginger Fox.

***

"Mrs. Sterling, you are the widow of the deceased?" Tonya asked Paula on the witness stand

"I am," Paula said. "We were married for almost five years."

"Would you describe your marriage as a happy one?"

"Successful would be more appropriate."

"You just heard Ginger Fox testify that your husband asked her to marry him. How do you see that as a successful marriage?"

"I know nothing about Ginger."

"You had no clue?"

"None."

"I find it hard to believe that a bright, sensitive woman like yourself had no idea that her husband was cheating, and he was about to divorce you. Women know these things."

"Mrs. Sims, my husband was well known for his liaisons with women. He took them to bed, yes, but never to the alter."

Tonya looked to see Victor come into the courtroom.

Victor strolled toward her. He handed her a blue folder. "Sorry for being late."

"This is it?" Tonya said, removing the document. She gave a quick glance.

"It was what we expected," Victor said.

"Mrs. Sims?" Judge Munford prompted. "Do you need a break?"

"No, Your Honor." Tonya focused on Paula. "Mrs. Spencer. You just told the court that you did not know that your husband was about to divorce you, but you did know about your husband's will." She held up a copy. "I have a copy of it right here from the District Court. I would like to have it marked as Defendants Exhibit D."

Judge Munford said, "If there is no objection, it is so ordered."

Stephanie walked over to look at the will. Without a word, she headed back to the prosecutor's table.

"This document makes you equal with your stepson," Tonya explained. "Do you know how many shares your stepson owned?"

"I'm not sure," Paula said.

"You have no idea?" Tonya asked. "What if I told you about fifty million?"

Paula gave a half-smile. "That sounds about right, but I'm not sure."

"But if your husband left you for Ginger Fox or another woman, your prenuptial agreement would only provide you with one million a year and you would inherit nothing."

"If you say so," Paula said in a dismissive tone.

"Would you say that you are better off with your husband dead than alive?" Tonya asked. "I mean, let's face it, fifty million is better than five million."

Stephanie jumped to her feet. "Objection. That is speculative, argumentative, and on top of that, Mrs. Sims is harassing her own witness."

Paula waved a hand in mid-air. "I really would like to answer if you don't mind."

"The court will allow it," the Judge said.

Paula opened her purse. "I knew that you would bring this up." She took out a document. "So, I came prepared. This is a copy of my husband's most recent will that he drew up." She handed it to Tonya. "His lawyer will file it before the end of the day. You see he gave it to me about a month ago."

Tonya looked over the document. She read where Montgomery Sterling left everything to his son, Spencer. She tried not to appear disappointed.

"Mrs. Sims, you will notice that my husband left everything to his son and not me," Paula said with confidence. "I inherit nothing from his death."

Tonya wanted to knock that smirk off her face. She may not have had her husband killed but she was still a despicable woman. She gave a weak smile. "I offer you my sincere condolences. I'm sure you are looking forward to another marriage. This time with your stepson. How convenient."

Paula's face dropped. She gave Tonya a hard look that could kill.

"Objection!" Stephanie yelled.

"Sustained," the Judge called. "Mrs. Sims, I realize that it has been a while since you were in a court room, but we will not have these off-color remarks," he scolded. "Do I make myself clear?"

"Yes, Your Honor." Tonya turned her back on Paula Sterling. "I have no more questions for this witness." She plopped down in the chair.

"You may step down," the Judge instructed Mrs. Sterling.

Victor leaned over her shoulder. "Tonya, check that attitude," he whispered. "You are losing it up there."

"I know you are right," Tonya said. "I couldn't believe it when she presented that will. I wasn't prepared for that."

Paula gave Tonya one last look before heading to her seat.

"She's a crafty one," Dominique said.

"Don't let her get under your skin," Victor said. "That's what she wants."

"Anything on Priest?" Tonya asked. "We have to do something quick. Mrs. Sterling is making me look bad."

"So far there is still no sign of Priest," Victor said.

***

Later that night, Victor carefully followed Priest as the vehicle drove along Interstate 295. A tip came in from the Virginia Police Department that the white Pontiac had been spotted at a Crown Gas Station in Springfield, Virginia. Lucky for him there wasn't much traffic. Priest crossed the Woodrow Wilson Bridge, the Anacostia River, and was now headed into Washington, D.C. His phone rang. He stuck the Bluetooth in his ear and answered. "Speak."

"Where are you, boss?" Paul asked.

"I'm trailing Priest into D.C.," Victor answered. "Why is he surfacing now? There must be a reason. No one has seen him in two days and suddenly he reappears."

He followed a few minutes more before making a right on Wisconsin Avenue. "He's heading to the news station." He followed the vehicle into the parking garage of WADC. "He's headed down to the basement. This has to have something to do with what happened in the courtroom today," Victor said.

"I agree," Paul said.

Victor turned off the truck lights. He watched as Priest parked, got out of the car, and hurried toward the door. He took out a key and let himself in. "He has a key."

"It all makes sense now," Paul said.

"Yes, it does," Victor said. "I'm following him."

"Be careful," Paul said. "Remember we don't have weapons."

"I won't need one." Victor ended the call. He made a dash toward the door. He took out a credit card, jimmied the lock, and quickly let himself in.

He found himself inside the stairwell. It was quiet. He tuned his ear to listen for footsteps. He heard one set. "That must be Priest," he said to himself. A door opened and closed with a loud bang. Taking two steps at a time, he made his way up the stairs in no time. He got off on the sixth floor. The hall was dark, except light coming from one of the offices. It had to be where he went.

Victor stepped behind the wall. He peeped around the corner. A moment later, Priest re-emerged. *He must have found what he was looking for,* he thought. When he passed, Victor stepped in front of him. Priest looked startled. "Don't you give up?"

"You know better than that," Victor said. "Found what you were looking for?"

"That's none of your business," Priest replied.

Victor held out a hand. "Give it to me. I'll let you live."

Priest chuckled. "Is this some kind of joke?"

"I don't joke," Victor said. "You killed Sterling Montgomery and Abbey Knowles."

"What of it?"

"Hand it over!" Victor exclaimed. "Now!" He covered the small space between them.

"I will hand over nothing," Priest said. "You will have to kill me for it."

Without another word, Victor's fist found the right side of Priest's face. He stumbled but managed to return a blow of his own. A hard fist to Victor's chest sent him crashing to the wall. He shook off the cobwebs. He looked to see Priest heading for the stairs.

Priest managed to open the door. Victor caught up to him and landed a karate chop to the back of his head. The force sent Priest tumbling down the steps. He landed in a heap at the bottom. He let out a loud groan as he tried to get up but fell back down.

Victor made his way down the stairs. Suddenly a door suddenly opened. A young woman appeared. She screamed in surprise at what she was seeing. Priest took the opportunity to escape, knocking her over.

Victor's long legs allowed him to reach the bottom of the stairwell in time to see Priest exit on the first floor. He caught up to him. He opened the door to sounds of gunshots fired at him. He crouched behind the door.

A moment later, Victor carefully and slowly reopened the door. He caught a glimpse of Priest rounding a corner. Again, he was hot on his trail. Once more, Priest shot at him. He took refuge behind a wall.

When he saw Priest run into the lobby of the station, he took off after him.

"Stop, right there!"

Instead of obeying, Priest pointed the gun at him. Two shots rang out of nowhere.

Victor dropped to the floor, but when he got to his feet, he found Priest face down in the middle of the lobby. He hurried over next to him. Blood was oozing from his face and neck. He placed a finger to his neck. There was no pulse; he was dead. He looked around trying to figure out where the shots came from.

Victor turned Priest over. He closed his eyes. He looked around to find something close to the body. It must have fallen while he was running. It was a black notebook. He picked it up, flipping through it. It was full of names and numbers. "I got you, you bastard."

***

"He's in no condition to talk," Detective West said thirty minutes later. "I thought we talked about this. Did you have to kill him?"

"I didn't kill him," Victor argued.

"Who did?" Detective West asked. "I never thought that this is the way that he would go. This is kind of sad, if you think about it."

"Couldn't have happened to a nicer guy," Victor replied.

"You said he had a key and let himself in?" Detective West said.

"I saw him with my own eyes," Victor answered.

"Paul, are you on the case as well?" Detective West asked.

"I do work for VSI," Paul answered.

"The agency is looking like it's going to be something," Detective West said.

"I think so, too," Paul agreed.

"Can we talk about the case?" Victor asked.

"Okay. Okay, about the keys. It could be there are a lot of keys floating around and many who have access to them. Quite a few people do work here," Detective West stated.

"Maybe," Victor said. "But he wasn't looking to steal or meet anyone. He went straight into Spencer's office. He came out a moment later. He got what he was looking for."

"What was that?" Detective West asked.

"I have no idea," Victor lied

"Neither do I. He can't tell us now, can he?" Detective West said. "On that note, I am out of here. I will see you guys in court." He walked off.

"You're not going to tell him about the black book?" Paul asked.

"When I'm done with it," Victor replied.

"That's withholding evidence," Paul said. "But I don't have to tell you that."

"No, you don't," Victor said. "He dropped it before he was shot. So, technically it's not evidence. We will examine it for a couple of hours and then hand it over. Come on, let's head back to the office."

Chapter Twelve

"Your Honor, we have come upon some new evidence that we would like to place into evidence," Tonya said the next morning. They were standing before the bench. "It is defense evidence number five." She handed the black book to the clerk. "With this evidence, it will clear my client."

"May I see it, Mrs. Sims?" Stephanie asked.

"Of course," Tonya said.

The clerk handed the book to the Stephanie. After flipping through it, she handed it back to her. "Your Honor, I'm done with the witness."

"Mrs. Sims," The Judge prompted. "I take it you have questions for the witness?"

"Yes, Your Honor," Tonya said. "I do."

Tonya strolled confidently to the witness stand. Spencer sat. A smug look on his face

"Mr. Sterling," Tonya began. "You are the only child and sole heir of Montgomery Sterling?"

"Yes, I am," Sterling answered. "Let me say for the record that I knew nothing of the will until my stepmother took it from her purse and presented it yesterday."

"Thank you for that," Tonya said. "Okay. You worked for your father. Is that right?"

"I was Vice President of the company."

"Such a large title but not much pay," Tonya pointed out.

"I was being trained to take over," Sterling said. "My father felt it's best to learn that way."

"You didn't have that much money, but you have a penthouse in D.C.?" Tonya said.

"Yes."

"A ski chalet in Aspen?"

"Yes."

"A beach house in Florida."

"Objection," Stephanie exclaimed. "What is the relevancy here?"

"Mrs. Sims, I have to agree with the Prosecution," Judge Munford said.

"That's okay, Your Honor," Tonya said, walking over to the defense table. Dani looked worried. "Don't worry," she whispered to her client. "I'm about to connect the dots," she said aloud.

"Make it quick, Mrs. Sims," the Judge scolded.

"Mr. Sterling," Tonya said, walking back to the stand. "How do you manage to live a champagne life without much money?"

"I inherited a lot of money from my mother," Sterling replied.

"You gambled it away," Tonya said. "Matter-of-fact, your father was very upset with your gambling."

"That's not true," Sterling argued.

"Your father despised your nasty gambling habit."

"My father told me to stop," Sterling said. "And I did."

"Your Honor," Tonya said. "I would like to show Mr. Sterling defense exhibit number five."

"Certainly, Ms. Francis," Judge Munford said to the clerk.

The young woman walked over and placed the black book in front of Spencer.

"Mr. Spencer, I would like for you to take a look at the black book in front of you," Tonya said. "Do you recognize it?"

Sterling shook his head, then said, "No."

"Are you sure you don't recognize it?"

"I already said that I don't," Spencer answered.

"Even if I told you the man that was shot last night took it from the desk drawer in your office?"

"I have never seen it before," Sterling argued.

'Okay, fine," Tonya said. "Let's move on. I want to ask you about your relationship with your stepmother."

Sterling glared at Tonya.

"If I were you, I would answer truthfully," Tonya said.

Tonya began walking up and down in front of the bench. "Now, is it not true that you and your stepmother are lovers?"

The courtroom went silent waiting for Spenser's answer. Everyone was on the edge of their seats in anticipation of the son's answer.

"Yes," Spencer finally answered.

The courtroom erupted in chatter. Judge Munford banged the gavel. "Another outburst like that and I will clear the courtroom."

"I can't hear you," Tonya said.

"Yes, we're lovers," Spencer repeated.

"You hated your father?" Tonya asked.

"Yes, I hated him," Spencer answered without hesitation.

Tonya continued, "You hated him so much, you wanted to humiliate him by making love to his wife, in his bed, and in his home."

"Yes, I did all of those things," Spencer answered. "Because, I hated him. But I didn't kill him. I didn't kill him."

Loud whispers could be heard throughout the courtroom.

"I have no further questions for this witness," Tonya said. "But I reserve the right to recall him."

"Ms. Bigelow," the Judge called.

"No questions," Stephanie said.

"You may step down, Mr. Sterling."

Spencer quickly made his way to his seat. This time, he sat in the back of the room instead of next to his stepmother.

"Mrs. Sims," Judge Munford prompted. "Do you have another witness?"

"Yes. Your Honor. The defense calls Jimmy Farmer to the stand," Tonya said.

The former journalist glanced nervously around the courtroom before finally making his way to the stand.

"Mr. Farmer, you were a sports news anchor for WADC, is that right?" Tonya jumped right in.

"That's right," Jimmy answered in a low tone.

"Can you speak up, please, Mr. Farmer?" Tonya asked.

"I said that is right. I was a sports news anchor for WADC," Jimmy said.

"You were at the station for ten years. You earned numerous awards for your work, am I right?"

"Yes."

"You were the best in sports news," Tonya said.

"I think so," Jimmy said.

Tonya handed Jimmy the black notebook. "Can you please examine the notebook?"

Jimmy took the book without fear. He flipped through the pages. "Okay."

"Have you ever seen it before?"

"No. I haven't."

"What if I were to tell you that the man that stole the book from Spencer Sterling's office is a hired killer," Tonya said. "He's the same man that killed Montgomery Sterling and Abbey Knowles."

"I still don't know," Jimmy said. "It's still just a notebook with a bunch of scribbling in it."

Tonya removed the book from his hand. "I wouldn't just call it scribbling. You can see each notation is very important." She flipped to a certain page. "Can you please read the first page?" She returned the book to Jimmy. "Five-thousand dollars. Ten-thousand dollars. Redskins. Cowboys. Eagles." He handed the book back to her.

"I believe the term is Round Robin," Tonya replied. "You know a lot about that, right?"

"I have no idea of what you are talking about."

Tonya handed Jimmy a copy of his personal bank statement. "Will you identify this bank statement for the record?"

Jimmy looked at the statement. "It's mine."

"Mark the statement as defendant Exhibit E." Tonya pointed to line on the statement. "What is this deposit?"

"Fifty thousand dollars," Jimmy answered.

"Fifty thousand dollars withdrawn from your bank account the day before Montgomery Sterling was killed. Suppose I was to tell you that the same amount was also deposited the day after he was killed."

"I don't know," Jimmy said.

"Coincidence?" Tonya said. "I don't think so. Mr. Farmer, I am sorry to have to do this, but you had him killed."

"No, I didn't."

"Yes, you did," Tonya argued. "You had Priest to kill Montgomery Sterling because he knew about your gambling habit. I mean, he loaned you money time and time again. He was a good friend to you or you thought he was until you found out that he was sleeping with your wife."

The courtroom gasped.

He closed his eyes. He leaned back in the chair.

Tonya looked over at Stephanie. Her mouth was gaped.

"Isn't that right, Mr. Farmer?"

"Fine, I will admit Mr. Sterling was having an affair with Cindy, my wife."

Tonya glanced back at the beautiful blonde woman sitting behind Paula Sterling. "You found out and had him killed."

"No. Like I said, I knew about it." Jimmy dropped his head. "My wife did it for me."

"What do you mean?" Tonya asked.

"I mean, Cindy knew that Montgomery had a thing for her," Jimmy began. "She used that."

"To get him to pay your gambling debt."

"Yes."

"It may have started out that way," Tonya said, walking up and down in front of the witness stand. "But then something happened that you never expected. Am I right? She fell in love with him and him with her." She glanced at Cindy. She lowered her eyes.

"That's not true!" Jimmy yelled.

"Yes, it is," Tonya replied. "Your wife told you that she wanted a divorce. You couldn't let that happen. After all, if she was involved with the victim, you could gamble as much as you wanted to. You're an addict. You pimped out your own wife to support your habit."

"I'm telling you none of this is true," Jimmy barked at Tonya.

"Do you know Priest?"

"Never heard of him."

"He knows you," Tonya said. "He kept some pretty interesting notes of his own. This will be Defense Exhibit F." She handed a stack of papers to the clerk.

"I would also like to see those papers," Stephanie said.

"In those notes, on the last page, it reads, 'Took care of witness Abbey Knowles for J.F.' Who's Abbey Knowles?"

"You tell me," Jimmy said.

"Alright, I will," Tonya said. "She is the young lady that worked in the Pawn Shop that sold the murder weapon to him. The same weapon that was used to kill Montgomery Sterling and was later used to kill her."

"So?"

"So, she was going to come forward and tell what she knew about the weapon, but she was scared off by Priest, "Tonya explained. "Priest told you that she was going to be a problem. You instructed him to take care of her for an additional fifty-thousand-dollars to keep her from talking."

"Lies. All lies," Jimmy said.

Tonya could see the color drain from Jimmy's face. He was beet red.

"Ms. Bigelow, do you object to this line of questioning?" Judge Munford asked.

"No, Your Honor."

"Continue," Judge Munford said.

"Thank you, Your Honor, "Tonya said. "Priest found out where Abbey lived. He waited for the right moment, and just like he did with Montgomery Sterling, he shot through the window."

Jimmy leaned forward in the chair. "I already told you, I don't know anyone named Priest. I know nothing about this Abbey person. So, why would I want her dead?"

"The same reason that you shot and killed Priest."

Jimmy's mouth dropped. "What? You're being ridiculous."

"I don't think so," Tonya said. "Abbey could link Priest to the murder weapon that was used to kill Montgomery Sterling." Tonya walked over and picked up the gun off the evidence table. She held it up. "This weapon. You couldn't afford to have Abbey alive; just like you couldn't afford to keep Priest around, knowing what you have done." She stood in front of Jimmy and looked him straight in the eyes. "So, you waited for the right moment and you shot him."

"You're on the wrong track," Jimmy said.

"I'm on the right track," Tonya said. "And I can prove it." She nodded to Victor.

Victor got up and stepped through the double door. He returned a moment later with Abbey in tow.

Jimmy frowned. "Am I supposed to know her?"

"That's right," Tonya said. "You two never actually met. Jimmy Farmer allow me to introduce Abbey Knowles."

The color drained from Jimmy's face.

"What's wrong, Jimmy?" Tonya asked. "You look shaken."

Jimmy jumped to his feet. "It can't be! She's dead."

"Oh, but it is," Tonya said.

Judge Mumford banged the gavel. "Quiet! Who is this woman?"

"Your Honor, this is Abbey Knowles," Tonya replied. "The woman that Jimmy Farmer hired Priest to kill because she could link him to the weapon that was used in the murder of Montgomery Sterling."

"But the news said she was killed," Judge Munford said.

"I know, Your Honor," Tonya said.

"Sidebar," Stephanie called.

"I think that's a good idea," Judge Munford said. "Approach the bench."

Tonya and Stephanie stood before Judge Munford's bench. He didn't look happy. "Mrs. Sims, you better explain what the hell is going on."

"Your Honor, we had to do it this way in order to keep Abbey Knowles safe," Tonya explained. "There really wasn't any other way."

"You could have thought of another way instead of misleading this court," Stephanie whispered.

"How did I mislead the court?" Tonya snapped.

"Quiet!" Judge Munford banged the gavel. "Mrs. Sims, who was the victim that was killed?"

"It was Ms. Knowles boyfriend, Your Honor," Tonya explained.

"Step back," Judge Munford instructed. "Is there anything else from the defense?"

"No, Your Honor," Tonya said. "That's all for the defense. Our job was to prove that Dani McCall did not kill Montgomery Sterling. I feel that we have done that. I make a motion to dismiss all charges against my client."

Judge Munford glanced over at the Prosecution.

"We second that motion, Your Honor," Stephanie said.

"Bailiff take Mr. Farmer into custody. All charges are dismissed against Ms. Dani McCall. You are free to go." The Judge banged the gavel.

The courtroom erupted into happiness.

Dani threw her arms around Tonya's neck. "You were wonderful. I can never thank you enough."

"I gave you my word," Tonya said. "It wasn't just me. It was a family thing." She began placing the papers in the briefcase. "I told you I was going to get you off. And I did."

"I think I'm going to cry," Dani said. "I don't think I could have made it through a trial. You are a Godsend."

Tonya picked up her briefcase. "I don't know about all of that."

"Will you be taking more cases?" Dani asked.

Tonya nodded. "I think so."

"I'm glad to hear that," Dani said. "I'm sure that Stephen will come around. He'd be a fool not to."

"Thank you for those encouraging words," Tonya said. "What about you? You're going back to work?"

Dani smiled. "I can't wait to get back in my chair."

"I look forward to seeing you back on the air." Tonya gave her sorority sister a hug.

"Send me a bill. I will send a check right over," Dani said.

"Make it out to VSI Investigations," Victor said, walking up to the ladies.

Dani giggled. "Will do. How about I treat all of you to dinner?"

"I know the perfect place," Victor said.

The group walked through the set of double doors and out into the corridor.

"It's media madness out there," Detective West said. "Prepare yourself."

"Can we go out the back?" Tonya asked.

"Give me a moment." Detective West began to turn away then paused. "Congratulations, Tonya. You haven't lost a step."

"I agree," Stephanie said. "I'm not happy that I lost." She cleared her throat. "But I'm happy to see you back in the courtroom where you belong. I look forward to going up against you in the future."

"Thank you," Tonya said. "It's good to be back. I look forward to going up against you again."

"Bring your 'A' game," Dominique said. "She's a Sexton." She and Tonya high-fived each other.

"If you need a good investigator," Victor said, "give me a call. I don't have a business card at the moment."

"No need," Stephanie said. "I know where to find you." She sidestepped the group and sashayed off.

"She was feeling you," Gerald said.

"Definitely," Paul added. He continued watching the prosecutor until she vanished from view. "She is something else."

"Look at us, the Sextons," Gerald boasted.

"And Lake," Paul added.

"Three good looking men in business together," Gerald said.

"And women," Tonya said. "Don't forget me and Dominique. We helped too."

Victor nodded his head in agreement. "Yes, you did. I admit it feels good to have my own agency. I want to thank you guys for everything that you did."

"Everything?" Gerald asked. "You weren't happy about how I got some of the information."

"We will talk about that later," Victor said. "There is a legal way to get the same information."

Gerald drew his eyebrow together. "What's the fun in that?"

They giggled.

"Paul, are you ready?" Victor asked. "This was just a warm up."

"More than ready."

Tonya walked back toward them. "Come on guys. We're going out the back."

"We're ready," Victor said.

The three men surrounded Dani.

"Are you ready for your next case?" Gerald asked.

"New case?" Victor asked. "What new case?"

"Didn't I tell you?" Gerald teased.

"No, you didn't."

"Will they need an attorney?" Tonya asked.

"Something tells me I am going to regret going into business with family," Victor said, walking out of the back door of the court house.

THE END

About The Author

Sammie Ward is an Author/Writer/Publisher who was born and raised in North Little Rock, Arkansas, and now residing in Maryland. She began writing Confessions short stories on the advice of a friend. Since then, she has written over sixty short stories, six novels, and one novella. She is published in fiction and nonfiction. To learn more about Sammie Ward, visit her website:
https://www.ladyleopublishing.net

Also By Sammie Ward

Novels

Love By Design (LoveStorm Romance) Coming 2019

Lasso (LoveStorm Romance)

A Little Hot Chocolate For My Soul (Anthology)
Lace & Honor (LoveStorm Romance)
Love To Behold (Novella)
It's In The Rhythm (Indigo)
7 Days (The Victor Sexton Series) Book 1
In The Name of Love (LoveStorm Romance)

Short Stories

Joseph The Dreamer
David The Shepherd Boy
Ruth the Faithful
A Touch of Magic
What Are Girlfriends For?
The Sweetest Thing
When Love Comes Around
A Line In The Sand
Weekend Escapade
Second Chance At Love
Sweet Island Temptation
Smooth Operator